Candle
Dancers

Candle Dancers

To

Jack a Breage.

Love

Neville

Neville Green

author*HOUSE*®

AuthorHouse™ UK Ltd.
1663 Liberty Drive
Bloomington, IN 47403 USA
www.authorhouse.co.uk
Phone: 0800.197.4150

Published by AuthorHouse 09/10/2013

ISBN: 978-1-4918-7752-4 (sc)
ISBN: 978-1-4918-7754-8 (hc)
ISBN: 978-1-4918-7753-1 (e)

To Sue

One

Dawn was emerging, accompanied by distant howling thunder. The dark brown sky had swirls of golden yellow, musty green, and purple cork-screwing through it.

The Majestic Casino, now renamed the Dick Doc Casino, with its Grand Theatre was on the edge of a vast mining town. Grisly, featureless buildings ran along litter-strewn streets and rutted roads.

The Grand Theatre was now a vast, cavernous black eyesore. The gilded ornate grandness had been torn out, gutted, and destroyed many years ago, usurped with the bland utilitarianism of the new age.

The manager of the casino, Strid Docker, had been pleased with himself. He had persuaded the director, Dix Dannering, the impresario of the variety troupe Candle Dancers, to bring his show for a mutually agreed cost to this hinterland, this forgotten outback on the planet Junios. The Candle Dancers would perform in the Grand Theatre, though Docker hadn't expanded on the grandness—or the lack of it.

When the Candle Dancers had arrived, there were no comments from them about the grandness, only quizzical looks. They had quickly settled in and started rehearsals; chaos reverberated, exchanges were angry, fragile egos screeched, and performers sulked. Then, when all problems were resolved, the rehearsals were completed and a wrap was called.

They were professionals. The show had kicked off on time, on schedule.

The theatre was packed to full capacity. The audience, mostly miners, had been enjoying the performances with appreciative laughter and booming applause, and then with good-humoured booing as they disliked the act that followed—a prissy act with two dancers prancing about. When they had completed their effeminate dancing, the miners showed their disapproval, shouting and jeering crudely and lewdly. They didn't want intellectual ballet crap—they wanted earthy, sexy, bawdy acts, something to enjoy and have a good laugh at, to forget for a moment their horrible existence.

It had happened quickly like the touching flash of live wires. The good humour turned sour, and the booming applause died. Now the audience were staring silently and disapprovingly towards the empty stage.

The word "shrites" had been screamed out, instantly stilling and silencing them. It was a word they hated, abhorred, feared, a slang word for the poisonous excrement of the miniscule knife-fly that inhabited and swarmed in the mines and drilled holes where they worked. It was detested. Some of them ducked down and looked around, fearful that a swarm might be in the theatre.

"Shrites, shrites!" screamed the comedian Estoppel Xit, a name given to him when he was a dirty, scruffy child by the late father of Dix Dannering. The words had been tattooed on the back of his scrawny neck. He was now springing onto the stage like a frenzied marionette with its strings twisted, the tails of his black evening coat flying out behind him. His buckled and bent skinny legs were clad in thin, tight, pin-striped trousers, and his shiny, cracked, patent leather clown shoes were clapping, flapping loudly down on the old worn stage boards.

"You moronic, uncultured, uncouth shrites!" Spittle and phlegm cascaded out of his mouth, splattering the frills of his dress shirt. "They were brilliant; they were fantastic!" He clattered and flailed down to the front of stage, thrusting his thin, crooked body over the flimsy, curved tin footlights that were once electrical but now held dripping wax candles with fluttering, flickering flames.

In that same moment, like the flecked brackish froth blown across the abandoned seas, the front row of the audience rolled and folded back, moving away from him, the legs of their iron chairs shrieking as they scratched the black metallic floor. They attempted to avoid the grey spraying spittle, and the ones directly below the spitting figure

2

tilted back too far, their chairs shooting out from under them. They fell backwards, crashing down onto the tables behind and sending the thin glasses of the expensive, lethal, head-banging liquor flying.

In that one catalytic movement, the audience in the casino's dark theatre erupted into a sprawling squall of bodies, fighting to keep upright to protect not themselves but their drinks from being spilt.

This didn't deter Estoppel Xit's flow of invectives and insults, and he used them to emphasize the incredible stumbling clumsiness and loutish behaviour of the bawling, squirming mass of white faces below him. "What's your right, shrites? Look at you, look at you! Not one asshole of you can dance like they did. They were superb—the total embodiment of beauty and passion." He leered at them. "Pathetic, pathetic. You take the piss, then you deserve it."

He straightened his arched back and flung back his tailed coat. His gnarled, thin fingers grabbed the top of his striped trousers and started to grapple with the hooks and eyes that held the flies together.

The audience turned en masse, attempts to rescue their drinks forgotten. Their stomping, kicking, shouting, and cursing stopped, and they looked silently at the stage, at Estoppel Xit's old, bent figure prying open the front of his trousers in the flickering light of the stage's foot candles.

Dix Dannering was standing at the prompt desk in the corner of the stage's wings. But now Dix Dannering's eyes weren't glued to the cue sheets to follow every music beat, every lighting cue as they would have been. Now, his face was squeezed tight into a grimace, his top teeth biting hard into his lower lip. Now he was watching Estoppel Xit.

He had never seen the man so angry, never seen him so malevolent towards an audience. Yes, he always abused them, always taunted and berated them; it was part of his act, and everyone knew it, accepted it, welcomed it, even paid to see it. People felt cheated if he didn't do it with all his vitriolic enthusiasm. But this was different. This time Dix Dannering knew Estoppel Xit meant every word, every syllable of every word, every spitting invective—and he knew the audience knew instinctively that it wasn't his act. These insults were real and were meant for them.

Dix had watched slightly bemused as Estoppel Xit had sprung onto the stage. It hadn't been scripted, and it wasn't in the running order. Babe Agol, the star of the show, was supposed to be next up. It was just after the acrobatic dancers, Zelta Christel and Mister Christel, had hurriedly and fearfully slipped into the wings after the jeers of derision. Mister Christel had slipped his arms round his daughter, swung her up, and had carried her with proud disdain quickly off the stage and into the darkness of the wings.

It seemed at that moment that Xit had cracked. His wry, distorted, lined face had stretched taut, and his blood-shot yellow eye had opened wide, practically bulging out of its socket.

Estoppel Xit had taken one brief glance at the dancers, and his face looked as though his heart had caved in. He became apoplectic with rage and anger, screeched out, and then hurled himself onto the stage and started his abuse.

Strid Docker had been in his usual, sacrosanct position at the bar, licking a water ice and feeling reasonably pleased. It was a good night, the casino was packed, and the miners had been extravagant in their spending. At first he had thought that the one-eyed comedian's screeching arrival on stage was just part of his act; he had even swivelled his enormous bulk around to watch. The moment Xit had started to undo the fly on his trousers, however, Docker knew immediately this wasn't part of the routine. He also knew when the squabbling and fighting stopped, and the miners turned silently towards Estoppel Xit, it was trouble—big trouble.

Docker slid his fat buttocks off his high stool, and with amazing speed and agility for a man of his strange and misshapen proportions—he had an enormous hump on his shoulders counterbalanced by a prodigious swelling of his stomach, long arms, gigantic hands and feet, and small bowed legs—he shoved and shouldered miners aside to get to the front of the stage. He swung himself up onto it, skipped over the foot candles, and hurtled across to Dix Dannering in the prompt corner, scattering the dancer's resin boxes.

"Get 'im off, or I'll git the police," Docker hissed, grabbing Dix Dannering's shoulder and spinning him around. "If he gets his pistol out, you're dead."

Dix jerked back and broke away, the stench of the bitter chewing grass on Docker's breath giving him the necessary strength and power to pull and squirm away from the grip. *If he gets his pistol out,* thought Dix, *it would be a bloody miracle.* He knew that Estoppel

Xit had a catheter tube and bag taped to his leg, his penis was like a withered twig—a result, Xit had told him, of being castrated as a boy at the catamite orphanage of the evil Tuns, once the most feared race of people in the galaxy, unmatched in their brutality. They had become extinct, eradicated by a more powerful force and its lust for power.

Xit had escaped by clawing his feet out of the leg irons, slithering through sewers, hiding by day, and running at night till he had found a space drome and a ship being cleared for lift-off. He found an open hatch into the stowage area; the ship's name was *Auriga Lick*, and its plate number, five zero zero three, was stencilled in large black letters above it.

Stage hands doing their final check on the costume skips, baggage, and scenery before securing the large brushed steel doors had found Xit—a fierce, feral, spitting scratching, small, stinking creature. They threw a painted floor cloth over it and brought the squirming bundle to Dix's father, who, against all the laws of the thirteen Galactic Nations, decided to let him stay rather than having him immediately returned to the master state from where he had escaped. After several times of being asked his name, he had finally muttered, "Little bugger. That's what them called me." A tattoo, a thin line of scrawled black letters and possibly a number, had been discovered on the back of the boys neck.

"Estoppel?" Dix's father read curiously. "And X I T. A number?" he queried. No one knew. "He has to be called something, he has to have a name." He closed his eyes briefly before snapping them open. "He might as well have that one—Estoppel Xit. That's what he'll be called." He added with a laugh, "Not marquee, never see it up in lights, but it's not bad."

He ordered Xit to be instantly entered in the ship's log under the crew's muster roll as ship's boy, back dated to an earlier time. It would give him security; Dix's father was rarely challenged, but just in case there was a search for him, he felt the boy would be safe.

Dix, up to the moment of Xit's entrance, had been pleased with how the show was going. The so-called orchestra—playing in the wings opposite him, not from an orchestra pit because there were no orchestra pits in casinos theatres – were two young men named Lrac and Sivad. Lrac was tall with a burnt umber face and eyes of black polished marbles. Sivad was squat and rotund with a bleachedwhite face and pearl eyes that rarely opened. They had been reasonably compos mentis, presumably because they had failed to find a supplier in this forgotten outback of the bacula bulbs they normally chewed, and although they had no sense of tune, they hadn't hit a wrong key on the synthesizers all evening, following all the cues and intros at the right moments.

Dix himself had given a pretty reasonable performance, getting the right responses at the right time. Even his joke had gone down well; it was always good to play both parts, even though it meant playing sideways to the audience, breaking the strict rule that you must always face and engage them. His costume had been specially designed for this, split lengthways from collar to turn-ups with one half red and the other half green. Face and head make-up, gloves, and shoes matched the costume.

"*I'm cursed because of my wife—cursed!*" He jumped round to face the other way and looked up. A quick lighting change brushed his face with red or green.

"What's wrong with her?" He asked as he jumped back the other way and looked down.

"*She doesn't know how to drink, and she doesn't know how to play cards!*" he said, spinning round again.

"That's not a curse that's a blessing. Why are you complaining?" back again.

"*Because she* does *drink and play cards.*" He twisted only his head, now under-lit with bright white light to face the audience. He grinned grotesquely as applause and laughter filled his heart. When he had introduced the chorus girls, and he gave his quip about each and every one being a freedom queen whose beauty was in the eye of the beholder—if, he emphasised, they'd sunk seven glasses of expensive liquor. This had got a cheer, a roar of laughter, and a scowl from Docker.

Irma, the solo novelty dancer, had been particularly good, dancing with lithe and sexy enthusiasm. Dix had even noticed Docker drooling and breaking out into a sweat as he watched her provocatively wrap and slide her long, sinewy body against the large, erect phallic candle symbolizing the generative power of nature. Even the scenic prop penis had worked well for a change, ejaculating on the right cue, gushing and erupting out of its heart-shaped top edible paper flowers the size of dinner plates, each one sprinkled with a tincture of marble liquor that the extractors and hole drillers loved. They had roared and shouted their approval at this spectacular ending. Some had even tried climbing onto the stage to grab Irma after she had slithered down the shiny metallic penis to take her bow. She had repulsed them with a flick of her skirt, sending them flying backwards in painful amazement with aching heads or broken noses, not knowing what had hit them, not knowing that the hem of the seductive, black, flowing skirt concealed flat, circular steel magnets sown into it to make it spin and spiral out up above her waist to reveal her white pants as she danced. They were magnetized to hold her onto the metal cladding when she slithered and coiled up and round the huge phallic candle.

The amorous stage invaders reeled and toppled back off the stage like rag dolls, having been felled with the hem of Irma's skirt, but they looked as though they had swooned from the exaggerated kiss that she had blown at each of them. This always received an enormous round of applause from the rest of the audience as Irma did an arabesque then a pirouette before leaving the stage briefly before returning to take another curtain call. On the third return Dix signalled by pulling his flattened hand across his throat for her to cut any more calls, and he then signalled to Lrac and Sivad to cue with a musical intro the following act.

Jollity Strad was the gurning gloom-pot comedian, wearing a large cap and a long, buttoned up to the neck, orange woollen coat. He appeared hesitantly and backwards, as if lost, and then turning round, squeaking with surprise as if seeing the audience for the first time and then recovering and chatting to them as if he had known them all his life. He held them with his laconic humour, mesmerized them with tales and stories with very intimate and embarrassing details. None of it was true, but it was believed by the audience, who cried in sympathy and laughed with relief, ending his act with death always being the happy final tag.

Perhaps on reflection, thought Dix, *I should have switched the line-up and brought Strad on after Popablu.* Popablu was a very pretty boy crooner with feline good looks and oiled hair the colour of polished teak. He was gifted and precocious, and Dix was convinced that Popablu was the Galactic Entertainment Corp's spy; it was said every troupe had one. He also hadn't liked how the pretty boy creep had used the two chorus girls. They had often been to Dix to tearfully complain that the boy had told them he loved them, but all he had wanted was sex. Dix had told them to stay away from him, that he was evil and desired adoration and could never resist belittling an inferior. But Dix always defended the slime ball, and he would until he found out for definite what his relationship with the Corps was. He had to be careful—they could disband the Candle Dancers with a snap of their fingers if they felt there was any dissension.

But the show was working beautifully—right up to the finale of Mister Christel and Zelda's routine. They had been perfect as usual; even the most hardened cynic should have been moved by their perfect timing and the practically impossible lifts, with both of them spinning and flying up and off the stage with amazing leaps. Their dance routine started slowly, with Mister Christel pretending to show Zelta a few basic dance steps as though she was an absolute beginner. This developed into an amusing and competitive dance, and then into a duelling sequence when each attempted to outdo the other with soaring jumps and turns of impeachable precision. There were complicated steps that developed into an incredibly fast movement, becoming even faster and almost impossible to follow. Finally they finished in a spinning trapeze movement that had Zelta flying backwards, up from behind Mister Christel, over his head, and out into the audience, to be caught at the very last moment by her ankle. Both of them then froze rigid in this impossible sculptural position, Irma's jet black shimmering hair cascading over her flawlessly pretty face, her head and arms flung back. This routine normally would have had the audience gasping in silent amazement before bursting into thunderous applause of appreciation.

It hadn't happened this time. The audience hadn't been impressed—they had only focused on Zelta's perfectly formed body and petite breasts that were thrust out towards them, though not provocatively or with any sexual intention. It was simply part of the artistic sculptural pose, as if both of them had been carved out of a block of bright, polished lignite. This statuesque position was normally held till the applause had started to die and the spotlights that had tracked them through the whole routine clipped off, leaving a final image, an etched negative impression on the retina of the eyes of a crystal white lightning flash that had been captured and held in time.

The shouts and roars jarred and punched Mister Christel in his guts. He was mesmerized, unable to comprehend the roaring, angry noises, and he intuitively spun Zelda with a flick of his wrist back onto the stage. The moment her feet touched, he put his arm round her glistening black shoulders, swinging her up into his arms and walking jerkily, as if his legs had short-circuited, not responding to commands or signals from his brain. The spotlights hesitantly following them into the wings before flickering off.

"It's the police, ye bastard, it he's not off this minute," yelled Docker, his face blistering red.

"He's off!" screeched Dix, moving quickly onto the stage as an iron chair flew across it, spearing the backcloth inches above his head. He grabbed Xit by the tails of his coat, swung him round, and released his grip. Xit flew across the polished wooden stage to land in a crumpled heap like a black oily rag at the feet of Docker.

How Dix avoided being hit by the barrage of flying glasses, metal tankards, and chairs being hurled onto the stage, he never knew. Perhaps it was the pure instinct of an old professional hoofer that had helped him pirouette through them and off into the darkness of the wings. He arrived just in time to stop Docker from banging Xit's head on the floor. Docker screeched, "You little fucker, I'll fucking kill you!"

"Stop it!" Dix yelled, grabbing Docker's huge, fat, knuckled white paws. "Take your hands off him, you moron. I'll deal with him."

Docker let go, throwing up his hands. Xit's head jerked back and, with a skull-cracking crunch, hit the scratched, black-painted floor.

"And you'll deal with that lot, will you? They're reeking up the bloody place," Docker shouted above the noise of angry bellowing, the crashing, clanging metal and shattering, exploding glass.

Dix put a hand gently round Xit's head and raised it up. Xit's eyes fluttered open. "He'll deal with it," he shouted back up at Docker, wiping away spittle from the side of Xit's chin and softly stroking the blemished, pale skin.

"Him?" choked Docker. "Him, that thing? Fuckin' not letting him do fuckin' nothing. I want him fuckin' out."

"It's the only way, if you want them to calm down," Dix screeched. Then he put his mouth to Xit's ear and whispered, "Sing."

Xit opened his eye and tried to focus on Dix's head and beak-like nose. "Sing?" he murmured, his eyelid flickering.

"Sing," Dix whispered again. "The song."

"The song?" whimpered Xit, gasping for breath. Dix slipped his hands under the arms of Xit and started to raise him up. "Now?" gulped Xit, swallowing the phlegm that was clogging the back of his throat.

"Now." Dix pulled him upright, kicking the crippled leg to untangle it from the stronger one.

Xit squeezed his eye tight, brought up a long and bony finger to flick away a speck of glass from the liquid crystal ball of his other eye, licked his tongue over his top and bottom teeth, opened his creased purple lips, took a deep breath, reached down into the depths of his lungs, and started to sing.

The first note, long and clear, seemed to pierce through the howling crescendo and the thunder of angry voices. Docker staggered back, shaking his head in disbelief. The first note, as the purple lips opened wide and a pinkish glow began to seep back into them, seemed the purist sound that had ever been heard. The first word that followed stilled the rumble and shuffling of the audience, who silently looked around, confused, searching and wondering from where such a beautiful, powerful, angelic voice was coming.

After the first line, Dix slowly manoeuvred Xit onto the stage, side-stepping the shards of glass, steel tankards, and iron chairs. He led Xit down to the centre and to the line of guttering foot candles. The audience looked at them squinting, disbelieving their ears and their eyes. They crowded, slowly, silently forward for a closer look. It seemed impossible for the voice to belong to such a body.

If any thought had pervaded their minds, it would have been how, out of such a decrepit-looking thing and out of such a foul mouth, which only moments before had been spitting and cursing them with the crudest words, there could now be such a beautiful sound. But no such thought entered their heads. They were enchanted, entranced, captured in hearts and minds by the song.

Xit had transformed into a beautiful boy with an angelic face the moment he had started singing.

Dix slowly and quietly left the stage, fading back into the gloomy darkness of the wings.

"How is this possible?" babbled Docker. "How?" He was transfixed by the crooked, hunchbacked figure. "His voice is . . . is . . ." He stopped, leaving his mouth open, his lips curled back over his large, green-stained teeth.

"The sweetest sound you have ever or will ever hear in the galaxy," whispered Irma Iggy breathlessly, having run down the two flights of stairs from the dressing rooms upon hearing the first note through the stage's tannoy system. After pulling on a bright green dressing gown and swaddling her hair in a towel, she had shouted to the others, who were packing the skips and trunks, to stop what they were doing. "Estoppel Xit is singing," she had yelled excitably.

They all immediately stopped their work and followed her, squeezing into the small space of the wings and hardly daring to breathe in fear of not hearing every word, every cadence. Some closed their eyes and bit their lips, tears glistening down their faces. Even Popablu, who had squirmed in close to the front had moisture creeping along the edge of his long, burnt orange eyelashes.

"Shush," hissed Jollity Strad at Irma, who was trying not to breathe. Strad held a shaking, long finger to his mouth and then moved his hand to cup round his white pointed ear.

Except for Xit's voice, all other sounds had stopped. It seemed that even the shrieking wind had died away, no longer heaving and tearing at the casino's corrugated steel roof. The long, red-necked, iron-beaked, emerald scavengers usually pecking the rotting food in the refuse bins had given up screeching and squawking and were now silent.

Babe Algol, the top of the bill star, was the last to arrive down from her dressing room, and she had squeezed her huge bulk into the remaining space, her large bosom drawn in, not wanting her panting breathing to interrupt one note of the song. Stagehands and technicians had drifted around Lrac and Sivad, who were listening with mouths wide open. Others, fly men and riggers, were leaning over the rails of the fly floor high above the stage like baked black buzzards on a wire, silently listening. All were held by the perfect sound of Xit's voice and the words of the song.

The words told of a planet where the air was clean and sweet, and the land was fertile. Rivers and lakes held sparkling pure water, the suns warmed and nourished the earth with golden light, and silver moons controlled and calmed the seas. The seas were filled with shoals of every type of succulent fish. Trees dripped with the freshest fruits every day of the year. The earth yielded food with little cultivation. Soft, gentle, clean rain swept over the land, and winds cooled and caressed the lush vegetation, from the snow capped mountains down to the shimmering seas.

The song told of the precious crystalline iridium mica that folded away from the rocks, and of the magnificent zircon hyacinth scattered along the virgin white sands of the beaches, climbing up to the crystal sharp, blue, snow-covered mountaintops that sparkled in daylight and glowed at night. It was a paradise where the elements, humans, and creatures were in total harmony.

The song ended with a rising crescendo that told everyone listening that this land could belong to them and was waiting for them. The songs expression of this arcadia, this utopia, was totally opposite to what the casino's audience, the waiters and staff, the members of the troupe, and every inhabitant of the galaxy had ever experienced. Perhaps some had a vague memory of being told what the planets were once like—a historical reference that had no relevance to them now.

Now everything, every element, even down to the smallest, the most microscopic particicle on every planet, was against them and threatening their existence. The galaxy was dying, and in its death throes it seemed to be purging itself of the virus that had scratched and drilled into it, polluted it, and poisoned its earths, seas, and air. The virus was still scratching and drilling, unaware (and perhaps uncaring) that they were responsible for the death of the planets.

The audience filling Docker's casino were the extractors, the miners, and the hole drillers who had to work in the dangerous, filthy veins and shafts hundreds of kilometres below ground, digging out the precious crystalline mica that was so important for the energy needed to create the food and water for the inhabitants of the planets. The shafts, veins, bore holes, and mines were plagued by miniscule knife-flies whose excrement, or shrite as it was universally called, could burn into the skin and seep into the blood, transforming and being reborn into microscopic larva worms that swam through the adopted body, squeezing out of eye sockets, creaking, and squeaking out of the aural cavity of ears or swimming downwards to exit, burning and stinging with searing pain from the penis or anus. The double-headed queens invaded and colonized the brain, slowly feeding off it. When this happened, the victim would become euphoric, as if with inebriated happiness. This feeling lasted for only a few hours, and then deep, dark, malevolent, psychotic madness developed. If the victim was lucky enough to be detected—lucky for both them and the rest of workers—they were killed, quickly bagged, and incinerated.

Under their normal clothes, the miners wore a shiny white ceramic fibre covering like an outer skin to protect themselves; this made their natural skin shrivelled like bleached white prunes. The helmets they had to wear were guaranteed to have a greenhouse effect on any pimple or spot, enlarging them to enormous, enraged proportions. None of the miners were teenagers or pubescent adolescents; none of them ate or touched anything known or thought to cause dermatological diseases.

None of the planets offered any comfort to their inhabitants. Barren deserts were swept by poisonous gassy winds, and in frozen wastes, if, by accident or design, anyone left the synthetic, air-conditioned environments they lived and travelled in, it was instant death by choking or by freezing and then immediately splintering into millions of ice particles.

All air, food, and drink was now filtered, refined, or manufactured in massive laboratories. A few arboretums, orangeries, and natural food conservatories and farms existed, but these were only for the most powerful and wealthiest of the galaxies denizens, the rulers who could dine on fresh fish, red meat, and organic vegetables.

Xit's song was about an imagined land. It had touched the hearts and minds of the hardest, most cynical of them. Was it a figment of Xit's imagination, or was it possible that such a place existed? This was the question that others who had heard the song before had asked. And now the casino's audience, the staff, and a few members of the troupe who had never heard it before wanted to have an answer.

Xit released the final, triumphant note, snapped his mouth closed, and stayed still, hovering above the candles. He was bent, twisted, and silent, his useless leg splayed out from his body, and his elongated shadow flickered grotesquely on the dirty mushroom-coloured cyclorama behind him.

The song seemed to linger, conjuring up the final image of golden sunlight flashing on crystal clear, sparkling pure water. Even when the sound had totally died away, this image was still retained, shimmering and flickering in the mind, glazing the retina of the eyes until it slowly faded into the harsh, dirty reality of the black cavernous theatre and the people's desperate lives.

Everyone was brought back to the casino with its hermetically sealed metal walls, the black iron furniture slowly corroding away from the toxic gases that had seeped in and permeated the air through the casino's air conditioning system. The workers were brought back to the squeaking outer skins that constantly reminded them of the shrite and of their wrinkled, crinkled bodies. They were brought back to their pitiful existence, endured to provide the meagre wages for their families to survive. They looked at Xit, now back to his original, decrepit, deformed, twisted self, standing silently and staring down at them like the physical embodiment of a question mark.

The audience wanted desperately to have an answer, and they squirmed and squeaked closer to him. They whispered the question, and when there was no response from Xit, they screamed and shouted it in all their different mother tongues. "Did it exist? Was there such a place, a planet?"

Xit stood straight, the question mark became an exclamation mark, and then he held his arms out and leaned towards them like a praying mantis, flapping his gnarled, yellowing hands and beckoning them to come even closer to him.

They all crowded nearer and tighter.

Xit held his hands up, closed his fingers except for the two index fingers, turned his hands slowly, and pointed at his mouth. Then he quickly stabbed them into the corners of his mouth, forcing his lips up into a horrible, horrendous grimace.

The audience shied back, and Xit released his fingers and with a croaking barking laugh rasped out, "Cretins. A shrite song for shrites, composed in a septic bog house when the bastard belly pox was erupting." He stabbed his gnarled, bony fingers at the pale, smeared cream faces below him before turning and screeching as he skipped along the line of fluttering flames, the shadow emphasising his bent, crippled frame.

"Sunlight that doesn't burn you to a black cancerous pulp? Water that doesn't make you vomit? Mica that folds away from rocks?" He stopped briefly to stare down into the wide open eyes peering up at him, tapping his clown shoes up and down, quicker and quicker. He suddenly stopped, and silence echoed round the cavern.

"Sunlight." He illustrated his words with actions, holding his head back as if up to the sun and fluttering his fingers as if they were the sun's rays. He coughed and crumpled down into a shrivelled black heap, his fingers still flickering round his face, and he gave a gurgling hiss. "Burning black, cancerous pulp." He sprung up. "Water." His hands swept down as if to scoop up water, bringing them back up to his mouth and drinking with gasps of appreciation, his tongue shooting out to collect the last drops and then retching, "Radiation that boils your intestines." He mimed vomiting, spewing, snorting out grey phlegm before wiping his mouth to hiss, "Mica," making the squeaking sound of the miner's inner suits before pretending to peel back the mica from a rock, holding it up to his eye to examine it, a smile of exhilaration spreading across his face before he gave a victorious yell. "Yes!"

He turned quickly and hurled the pretend mica into the sad, bewildered faces staring up at him, before freezing perfectly still and silent for a moment. He wheezed, "When the shrites are squeezing into your brains." He whispered, "Brains." Then louder, "That's when you'll see it." Screeching. "That's when you morons will ever see it." He squeezed his eye into a tiny slit, staring at them, coughing a ball of phlegm, and rolling it round in his mouth. He pursed his lips and then jerked back his head as if he was going to spit it at them, and as they reeled back, he dropped his head back and swallowed the phlegm, rasping out another barking, sarcastic laugh before turning and limping off, dragging and scraping his withered leg through broken and smashed glasses.

Everyone who had just heard the song for the first time still retained a golden, shimmering, sparkling imagery, a dream of pureness in their hearts and minds. Even though Xit had tried hard to sour and destroy it, the song had converted them. No amount of obscene, verbal desecration would persuade them otherwise.

"Why?" Irma Iggy sighed to Dix as she linked her arm through his. "Why does he always do that?" She watched Estoppel Xit push his way through the troupe, muttering gleefully to himself. "White horses riding the golden tracery of the seas, load of old bollocks, rank urine with the tracery of red gore."

Dix had heard and seen it before. It seemed to give Xit some kind of sadistic pleasure, as though he was getting back for being a twisted cripple. *Was the song about him?* reflected Dix, *What he should have been—beautiful, straight, upright, pure? And the denouement, was that how he thought of himself now?*

"No," said Dix aloud, and then to himself. "Xit is the kindest, most considerate, the most beautiful vivid person he had ever known." He laughed, realising what Xit was about. "What an act, what an old pro. They all believed him. Even I did, sort of."

In his mind he heard his father shouting at the acts, "And when you make your exit, keep your act going six steps into the bloody wings, even up to your bloody dressing room." Dix laughed again.

He sensed Irma's arm and unwrapped it; he didn't answer her question and shivered in disgust at her familiarity, annoyed that she was constantly trying to hold and touch him. He felt brittle and knew she was desperate to be intimate with him again. Whenever they were alone together, she would tell him how she envied his intelligence, how she found him beautiful.

It didn't flatter him. He accepted that he was reasonably intelligent, but beautiful? A bald head, piggy eyes, a long and protruding nose, a slice of lips offered above a thick square jaw, a flabby body with long arms, and legs tied to it like a badly made doll? Not in anyone's wildest imagination could he be considered handsome, unless they were barking mad. He did think Irma was a touch barking and therefore was never too severe or sharp with her, often giving her a weak smile and a nod as he moved away from her. But this wasn't the only reason he tried to keep a distance between them. He acknowledge that she was strikingly attractive—a bleached face gashed with brilliant red lipstick, studded with two orange and green rimmed melancholy eyes, shining with unnatural brilliance outlined with heavy jet-black liner, and framed with rigid, straight pink hair. She was tall and thin with amazingly long legs, and her breasts were like opaque balloons not fully blown.

She left him cold. Nothing about her aroused him, and he had often wished it did, because it would make his life simpler. One of the reasons he kept her in the troupe was because of her superb dancing; otherwise he would have found away to ask for a replacement years ago. She irritated him, and what irritated him even more was that he felt irritated *by* her, especially when it was nothing to do with her.

He knew it was his guilt that scratched and poked his subconscious. She was innocent and had no knowledge of his guilt or why he had it. His irritation was a gnawing anger at how despicable he felt and at how he should have known intuitively that making love to her years ago—even though it was intense and memorable, their kissing long and hard, he without the necessary skills, their love-making crude and clumsy; he still held it in his imagination—was wrong, hideously wrong.

He had once, when he was younger, carefully asked Xit, hinting at what he wanted to know. "Was Irma . . . ? No, I mean not that. Did Dad . . . you know . . . make, perhaps with Irma . . . ?"

Xit laughed. "The governor liked the ladies."

"I was, you know, just wondering about who my mother . . ." he let the question trail away.

Xit quizzically raised his eyebrow. "You thinking of getting off with Irma?"

"No, no, absolutely not." He felt a hot flush rising up his neck. "No, I was just—it's not important. Bit too old for me, anyway."

"Still a good looker." Xit nodded and winked conspiratorially.

Dix grinned. "She couldn't possibly have been any . . . ?" He tried to convey his thoughts telepathically to Xit and it seemed to have worked.

"Relation?" Xit replied, and then he thought for a moment, looking at Dix as though he was a tailor sizing up a customer. "No, not possible, I would say. Can't think there could be, but my memory isn't what it was. But with your dad, who knows who it could have been? Lots of them, all sadly gone now, except Irma and Babe." He pulled at his bottom lip thoughtfully and then said, "Don't think it would have been Irma, not with Babe hovering. She'd have bitten his head off—well, more likely his pecker if he tried anything." He nodded his head as if remembering them. "Others, but not Irma. She's not the brightest star, but she's savvy and would have taken precautions. That is, if your dad did ever try it on with her, though she wasn't his type. Much too young. He preferred the more mature and experienced ones."

Dix felt he had got nowhere. The possibility that it could be Irma was still gnawing. He wished over and over that she would leave of her own accord, but she had always turned down any offers she received from other troupe producers.

17

He had accepted the guilt and the blame that he had unwittingly made love to his . . . He could never bring himself to say the word. He knew it would be with him forever. When he had first realized the possibility of this, he had immediately suppressed any desire for sex, and any desire or thoughts to masturbate were instantly dismissed, the pleasure avoided by thinking about something else no matter how trivial—a loose caster on a chair, a worn rivet in a bulkhead. He avoided any possibility of being involved with anyone, and gradually over time, the desire, the lustful thoughts and feelings disappeared. He had neutered himself.

What he hadn't accepted was the physical personification of it, and this made him even more irritated and intolerant. He attempted to avoid looking at her or making any contact with her physically. Occasionally he had to look and have physical contact, but this was professional, and he divorced his mind and any natural feelings away from his emotions, isolating himself. She was never Irma but always Miss Irma Iggy, a solo dance artist who needed direction. He was never Dix but was always Mr. Dix Dannering. He was the producer, the master of ceremonies, the manager of the troupe, the one solely held responsible by the Galactic Entertainment Corporation for the troupe. He was one who took the blame for any indiscretion, any misconduct, any misdemeanour, any mis—of any kind.

These thoughts pounded in his brain as he turned away from Irma to bark at the rest of the cast and stage hands still lingering in the wings. "Have you struck yet and loaded?" he said sharply. Then he turned back to Irma and said softer, "We have to be away from here by mid-dark to stay on schedule."

"Dix, please," she replied in her little girlie voice. She desperately wanted him to love her, to make love to her like he had done many years ago. She had never forgotten the ecstasy. He was handsome, and highly intelligent, and she adored his quizzical mind and how he never accepted anything on face value. She liked his body, though she knew he didn't because he was always making fun of it. Still, she loved to wrap her arms around him and snuggle up to hear the powerful beating of his heart, to cover his white eggshell head in kisses, to prise open his thin lips and feel her tongue pushing past his teeth. She longed to feel his long, strong fingers combing through her hair. She didn't know why he had suddenly rejected her, why he wouldn't speak to her except formally, why he'd become so elusive. She asked herself what she could have done to have him treat her like this. Perhaps it was their age difference? But that had never seemed to worry him in the past. A sharp slap on her back stopped her musings, and a hand pushing her away from Dix made her yelp out as Docker roughly elbowed her aside, and moved in front of Dix, and started to prod him in the chest with a knuckled fist.

"I'm deducting it from the fee." He nodded his huge head towards the broken glasses and chairs littering the stage. "Savvy, boy?"

Dix sighed and nodded. They needed as much work as they could get, and he didn't want to lose another venue, even though these outland casinos were crap. He had to be submissive, polite, and acquiescent; he couldn't afford to be discourteous to a casino manager because of their direct access to the GEC, who could—and would without any proof required, without any challenge—disband his Candle Dancers.

"I'll get it cleared, Mister Docker," Dix said, assuming a servile appearance while muttering under his breath. "So you just trip trap back to your sty and leave me to it."

Docker scowled. "I'm still deducting it. You're trouble, fuckin' trouble." He gestured towards the audience. "They don't come here to be insulted. They want to escape for a bit of pleasure, not to be made fuckin' pricks of."

"Nothing I can fuckin' say," Dix said, adopting the strange patois of the region. "Make ye change yer mind?"

"What?" Docker leant into him and put his hands on Dix's shoulders. It wasn't a threatening action, and he had a curious gleam in his piggy bulging eyes. "Get it cleared up, and we'll talk." He moved away into the corner of the wings.

Dix ordered the stagehands to clear the debris. If they were to leave on time, they had to start packing up immediately afterwards.

As soon as the stage had been cleared, stagehands and technicians left to the loading bays, and Docker moved quickly to Dix and gently stroked his face. It was a fearful and menacing action, and perspiration beaded on his face a moustache of sweat glistened on his top lip. "Just one thing might stop me deducting it," he said nervously.

Dix sensed he was about to be asked to do something or have something done that wasn't in the contract. He waited till Docker's huge, bull-like head swung round to see if there was anyone listening. "What?" he asked as Docker turned back and leered at him.

"That little girly will do it." He ran his tongue round his green teeth. "My office. Send her up for an hour."

"Which little girly?" Dix moved away from him, not suddenly but as though he was considering the request. He was in fact moving backwards to the off stage microphone and tannoy system. *If I can get him to say her name*, Dix thought, *whoever he wants to spend an hour with in his office, I can have this bastard and his licence.*

Docker shuffled with him. "That little black girly, with the beautiful little tits." He cupped his big red hands up below his sunken chest to emphasize it.

"Little black girl with the tits. Ah yes, Irma?" said Dix, knowing that it wasn't her that Docker wanted but Zelta Christel. A savage thought made him gasp. *Perhaps if it had been Irma, perhaps I might just have accepted.* He grimaced. *How could I think like that? Why do I want to hurt her, humiliate her? She was innocent, as I was until I found out, almost certainly found out.* A flicker of possible doubt still lingered.

"Not fuckin' Irma." Docker jabbed Dix in his stomach with a finger. "Fuckin' Irma not black, is she. Fuckin' black girl that danced." He was whispering angrily at Dix's stupidity and jabbing harder.

"What's her name?" Dix asked quietly, feeling the microphone pressing against his left shoulder. Then he hissed confidentially. "There's three black girls in the troupe. Which one do you mean?" He turned his head slightly to one side as though to hear the answer better.

"I don't know her fuckin' name. Zeelta, Zoolta, some fuckin' name like that," rasped Docker impatiently.

"Ah, Zelta, Zelta Christel." Dix sighed and smiled, knowing the conversation was being recorded and the whole troupe would be listening, glued to the dressing room's tannoy speakers.

Docker creased up his mouth and smiled back happy. Dix now knew who he wanted. He wound his large pudgy hands together in glee, in anticipation of the pleasure to come.

Dix asked, "And you would like this girl, Zelta, to come to your office for an hour?" Docker nodded eagerly, a trickle of saliva squeezing out of his grinning mouth. "For what purpose?" Dix smiled innocently the lining of his mouth was dry.

The trickle of saliva sucked back into Docker's mouth as he gasped, "For what purpose?" Then a spitting howl "You some fuckin' eejit? For what purpose? To fuck her!" He unwound his hands and jabbed hard again with his finger. "To fuck her. To let you off the deductions. Savvy, boy?"

"To fuck her," Dix said clearly and distinctly, wanting it to be heard simply with no shred of doubt, no possibility that Docker's patois might be given as a reason for misunderstanding. "Mister Docker, sir, you want a member of my troupe of Candle Dancers, known by the name Zelta Christel, to come to your office in this?" Dix held up his hands and looked about. "In this, your casino, the Dick Dock Casino?"

Docker nodded and squeaked, "Yes."

"Your office, which is . . ." He leant closer into Docker, confidentially but still keeping his words loud and clear. "If I remember correctly, up the staircase with the intricate filigree iron banisters and white marble handrail?"

Docker nodded enthusiastically. "Yes, yes," he said, as though he thought Dix was remembering the directions to give to the girl.

"Down a corridor with a mosaic floor?"

"Yes, yes."

"Through the double-clad, shiny steel doors embossed with the silver and gold Galactic Entertainment's Corps emblem, and into your office." Docker nodded enthusiastically, a roguish twitch making his thick lips into a smirk. "And what an office, lit with soft, pinkish light if I remember it correctly." He had only been in it once when he'd first arrived to sign the contract. He felt as if he had stepped into a boudoir of a wealthy courtesan; he had been speechless and experienced a feeling of detachment from reality.

Dix continued, closing his eyes as if to visualize the room. "A very large, smoked, glass-topped desk supported at each corner by two naked maidens with proud breasts, carved out of black marble and entwined with gold snakes."

"Yes. What does this matter?" Now Docker was a little impatient; the twitch had disappeared.

Dix slowly opened his eyes and waved his hand to hush him to be quiet. "I must tell Zelta this so that she knows how to present herself, savvy?"

Docker squeezed his eyes tighter into slits and gave a slight nod.

Dix continued. "Opposite the desk, an enormous red couch is strewn with brightly coloured cushions and set in front of three pink-tinted mirrors, each one having a candelabra in the middle. Another mirror is suspended from above with a blue glass chandelier in the centre. This is where you want to have sex with her? Where you want to fuck her?"

Docker's beady eyes stared at Dix. "Yes." The muscles on his face hardened into a grimace.

"And if she does that, then you won't deduct anything from our fee for the supposed disturbance that you said we had caused?"

Docker was agitated and snorted. "Yes, you fuckin' eejit, that's what I said. Now get her to my office. Prompt, no more verbiage. Savvy?"

Dix knew he had enough evidence to get a conviction and to have Docker barred from ever holding a casino licence again. He had broken a law of the Corps: "No casino owner was allowed to demand or to solicit sex, by whatever means, from any of the troupes performing in their casinos, male or female."

Dix knew the laws and rules by heart—he had to. He felt like giving a victory punch in the air but contained himself to a mere whispery smile. He had Docker, no matter how powerful Docker thought he was. Like all other casino managers, Docker knew that he was the front line of representatives, the diplomatic arm of the Corps, in a position that would certainly and automatically lead to be given a position on the board. Dix knew they still had to obey the law.

But managers like Docker consistently broke the laws and rules knowing that few would challenge them, and that if they were ever challenged, the all-powerful Corps would fight tooth and nail with a battery of lawyers to protect them—and more important, its own reputation. None of their front-line men, as the Corps liked to refer to them, could ever be known or shown to break their laws.

Unless there was irrefutable evidence that may, in some way, be detrimental to the reputation and security of the Corps.

Dix knew he had irrefutable evidence, but was it enough? Was it totally irrefutable? Was it enough to get the Corps to review its front-line representatives? The whole of the troupe would be witnesses; they had heard it through the tannoy system, and it had been automatically recorded.

Dix knew he could have a little bit of revenge on the great Galactic Entertainment Corps, even though Docker was only a casino manager. But he was one that was a representative and was the total embodiment in taste, manners, and culture of the Corps.

Dix considered the possibility that he might not have total irrefutable evidence. What if he was accused of entrapment, of engineering this incident? These thoughts blistered in his head. There was no way this bull-necked, piggy-eyed, ham-faced, coarse brute was going to squirm his way out of it.

Against his better instincts, a nagging doubt said he had to make certain. If he could make sure that this asshole would have his licence revoked, it might help other troupe producers to bring charges against other casino managers. It might be the pebble that caused an avalanche, which might tumble the mighty Corps off its perch.

Dix was getting excited. "And you know?" he squeaked, stopping to draw in a lungful of air to get his voice back to the right pitch and then speaking hurriedly, not stopping for breath. "And you know and understand perfectly that by asking me to suggest to this young girl, Miss Zelta Christel, that you wish—no, that you demand to have sex with her in exchange for not having any deductions made from our fee is . . ." He couldn't remember the legal terminology but knew Docker would understand the gist, "Is against the laws and legislation of the Galactic Entertainment Corporation? And if they were ever to hear of it, if they ever found out, you would have your licence revoked instantly?"

Docker looked startled and swayed back.

Dix knew instantly that he had gone too far, had overplayed his hand. He knew that when Docker stepped back, his bulging eyes peeled wide open and then instantly snapped back into red slits, his mouth opened, his lips curled back over his crimson fangs, he let out a snarling roar, he clenched a huge fist and raised it up behind his right shoulder, and then he shot the fist, with all his massive body weight behind it, into Dix's eyes.

Dix knew definitely that he had made a mistake, had overplayed his hand.

In slow motion he saw the clenched, huge, shiny, mottled pink fist with gleaming white knuckles thrusting out like four sun-bleached skulls—and the massive signet ring, scrolled and interlaced with iron and silver and set with a single, sparkling ingot of gold hammered and carved to represent the head of a serpent streaking at him, spitting out shards of light. It didn't curve or swing down but was shooting straight into the centre of his eyes.

He tried to spin away, but the microphone had caught in the shoulder of his waistcoat, and he thought he heard Docker call him "Fuckin' spy."

But that was his last thought as the crash exploded against the side of his head, before his eyes jarred against his skull, before a steel band wrapped and tightened around his head, before a white, pink, orange, blue, and purple iridescent rainbow and brilliant blue lightning crackled, piercing his brain and wiping his thoughts away to instantaneous nothingness.

Two

"His eyes moved." Those were the next words that Dix faintly heard, in the distance and barely distinct. He heard his name being called by several indistinguishable voices, and then closer was the sharper voice of Xit. He sensed the pungent brown breath reeking of liquor and stale, acerbic chewing root.

He tried to move away from it, but his head was too heavy; it felt as though a huge weight had been placed on the centre of his forehead, as if the steel band was still there. He tried to hold his breath to stop the stench penetrating his nasal passages. He heard a cry, a voice screaming, and he recognized it as Irma's.

"He's stopped again, stopped breathing! You stupid bastard, Xit you've killed him again!"

The rancid smell disappeared, and Dix let out a huge gasp.

"Still breathing, I think, Miss Irma," he heard Popablu's soft, velvet voice and smelt the perfumed breath closing in on him. He imagined the carefully groomed, oily brown hair and manicured fingernails, and the smooth, sculpted face. Popablu cooed softly, "It is possible he's still breathing. Mr. Dannering, can you hear me?"

Dix tried to analyze the perfume. He had smelt it once before but couldn't think where. *Honey and bitter almonds?* he asked himself, savouring the taste. *Yes, that's it. Honey and burnt bitter almonds.*

"Mr. Dannering, if you can hear me, you had a rather serious accident."

"Not a bloody accident," Xit interrupted. "Bloody attacked, viciously, by that bastard casino manager."

"Docker," Dix heard Irma add.

"Maybe Mr. Docker was the perpetrator, maybe not," Popablu whined judiciously. "We have to wait for the results of the inquiry before we know that for a fact. We aren't allowed to speculate or make any judgement. The weighing up of the evidence has to be adjudicated on."

Dix couldn't hear Xit's comment but he knew it must have contained a stream of invectives, given Popablu's reply: "If you think that irrational outburst will help his case, you'd better think again, Mr. Xit. It's your word against a casino's manager."

Dix could imagine the sharp, flashing glint of Popablu's eyes, turning them from bright blue to cold silver steel.

Dix knew Xit had replied but hadn't heard it.

"Listen Mr. Estoppel Xit, we have a man here who is . . ." The perfume moved away, and Dix tried hard to hear what was being said, but everything was silent until the sweet aroma drifted back. " . . . Your continual use of invectives isn't helping the situation or the decision I have to make. Let me make this perfectly clear once again: I am not on anyone's side."

Someone must have said something because the voice paused briefly before continuing. "Yes. Again and again I have told you that I heard the tannoy. I have listened to the tape, as we all have, but what was there to understand? How was it possible to make anything of it? I wasn't there. I wasn't on stage when it happened, and neither were any of you. There were no other witnesses except for Mr. Docker, who in his sworn affidavit—and let me emphasise, his sworn affidavit—that Mr. Dannering was hit accidentally by a counter-weight from the flying cordage that had not been properly secured." The tone of his voice had changed from soft velvet to harsh steel authoritarian. "Now, you all must return to your quarters. Mister Christel and I will tend to this matter. You shall all be informed of our decision."

Dix heard, or rather sensed, a murmur of dissent, and then there was silence. The perfume still lingered, so he guessed that Popablu and Mister Christel were the only ones left.

"*Return to your quarters*"? *That must mean we are on the* Auriga Lick, Dix thought. He was comforted by this thought, but another thought was nagging him. *What had Popablu said? That they had all heard the tannoy system and the tape recording, but they were unable to understand them or make them out.*

He screamed inside. *Why couldn't you bloody understand it? I couldn't have had it made it any clearer. It was all there. I tried to get more, tried to make it an open and shut case, and that's why I'm bloody here!* He sniffed back a sob and emphasized. *Why am I bloody here? Why couldn't you understand it? What was there to understand?*

He let darkness close over him for a moment before he started to analyse what Popablu had meant. *I spoke clearly, even interpreting what Docker said so that his patois was perfectly understood.* He became agitated. *Why hadn't bloody Docker been arrested, been interned? What bloody sworn affidavit, what investigation, what unsecured counterweight?"*

Nothing was making sense. The heavy smell of bitter almonds distracted his thinking, and he sensed the soft breath against his face. "Three turns of light left for him to regain consciousness. Anything else in your opinion we can do?" The voice was matter-of-fact. Dix didn't hear a reply; he wouldn't have heard it if it had been bellowed in his ear, because his whole being was concentrating on "three turns of light left to regain consciousness".

What does three light turns left mean? Dix questioned. *I was hit by Docker and then brought aboard the Auriga Lick. I presume I am in the sickbay, or perhaps I'm in my cabin.* He had no sense of where he was, and he couldn't identify the location. *Wherever I am, it doesn't matter. What does matter is this time span.* He attempted to work it out. *I know I'm not conscious, not in the physical sense anyway, so I am unconscious and probably in a coma. I know I'm breathing because Popablu told Irma he thought—no, he said he presumed I was. I'm not dead, or otherwise I wouldn't be thinking. That's a presumption. I know it's a presumption,* he answered himself. *But it's a universally held presumption, and one we must presume to be right, must suppose to be undoubtedly true. Cogito, ergo sum: I think, therefore I am.* He gave a small, rueful smile.

He didn't contradict himself because he didn't want to be distracted by this abstract, philosophical conjecture. He was in a coma and could hear, smell, and sense things, and that was that.

Now I am aboard the Auriga Lick. Are we still on Fevourios Two, at the drome, or have we left? He had no way of judging.

By law they should not have been able to leave, because the ship's activators would only respond to his command, but he, Xit, and Mister Christel had reprogrammed them so that if Dix was ever incapacitated, the other two could take over. Occasionally he had been known to drink a little too much, and this was one of the reasons for the other two having the information. It was necessary because of the tight deadlines they had to meet and the allocated flight time schedules between venues they were required to keep.

Unconscious and three turns of light left! His thoughts tumbled together. *What if I've been unconscious longer?*

What? screamed another of his voices. *Yes, listen. Not three, possibly longer, possibly a semester or two even, except for three turns of light.*

No, no that's impossible. But Dix knew sadly that it was infinitely possible. He knew that Xit was using the past tense when he spoke, knew that Irma's voice held a sadness, knew that the conversation hadn't been taking place soon after his confrontation with Docker.

He screamed out. *Shrite, no they can't. They have to keep me here. They can't just jettison me, they can't just follow the stupid regulations. I'm alive!*

The sweet, almond aroma broke into his panic, and he focused all his attention on the unemotional voice. "It is pointless to prolonged this any longer. We have extended the time period much more than laid down in the regulations. We have to assemble the crew. You agree that the scanner's prognosis is correct?" There was a beat of time, presumably for the answer. "Brain dead. A sad fact."

No, no you stupid runt! screamed Dix. *I am not dead! I can hear and think. I am breathing—you know that, you said it.* He tried with all his power to communicate. *Open an eye, open an eye.* He knew where his eyes were; he could feel them, sense them. He stopped thinking of anything else and concentrated his whole thoughts onto his left eyelid. *I will lift it open,* he thought determinedly. *Lift, lift.*

He felt it straining to open, felt the skin stretching, pulling away from the sticky wax that held it closed and then tore apart, sparkled like the birth of a newborn baby. *Yes, yes,* he yelled. *Yes!*

The scent of honey and bitter almonds made him gulp and gag, but he was elated. He could sense the smiles, the cheering, the applause. He was waiting for Popablu's reaction, for him to pronounce that he was alive.

Dix was also aware that there was another thought seeping into his brain: that if the eye was open, why was it he was still seeing the flashing stripes and bands of rolling colours? Why couldn't he see Popablu?

"Sorry," Dix heard Popablu's voice booming out. "Thought I saw a flicker of something in the left eyelid." The heavy, sweet smell seemed to press against his nostrils, it was so strong. "No, must have been the light from the scanner. Carry on, Mister Christel. I will not interfere again."

Interfere! screeched Dix. *Keep interfering—don't stop! Are you blind? My eye is open-look!* But he knew it wasn't, knew that with all his will power, he hadn't been able to change a thing. His eyes remained closed. From their assessment and the facts given to them by all the medical equipment and computer systems they had on board for detecting life, he was dead.

He snorted, and then he grinned cynically as an old joke came to him. "And all his life flashed before him, badly produced." Dix sighed and felt sad, though a smile of nostalgia crossed his lips. *Not all badly produced, only some bits and . . .*

"We are gathered here," Popablu was speaking again, his voice serious and stern. "All members of the Candle Dancers troupe and crews of the *Auriga Lick*, plate number five zero zero nine three in the time zone, recorded by the ship's computers Neural CCD and Neural DZV to take an official vote, as laid down in the articles of the Galactic Entertainment Corporations paragraph five, section four. The motion, which will be voted on, is whether we should prolong the life of Mr. Dix Dannering, manager, producer, friend, and colleague of all assembled here, now finally and irrefutably pronounced, by all the medical equipment we have at our disposal . . ." He paused briefly before emphasising, "Brain dead. All data, diagnosis, and psychometric analysis has been assembled, and the outcome of being clinically dead determined by the ship's medical officer, Mister Christel."

It can't be now. There hasn't been time—it wasn't that long ago. Dix tried to make an assessment of the time span, and a smile broke into his thoughts and then words. *How time flies when you're having fun. Shrite.* Xit's breath wafted over him. *I must concentrate on what is being said.*

"No definite proof he's brain dead, those fucking things can't be relied on," Xit cursed. "You can't rely on an analysis and diagnosis being determined by a fucking robot. He's breathing, for raptor's sake."

Dix smelt Xit's rancid, bitter, glorious brown breath wafting over him; he loved it, wanted to poke his tongue into it. "Oh thank you, thank you, you beautiful, sweet man."

The glorious odour disappeared, and the bitter perfume bit back. "The respirator is breathing for him. Without it he—" A deep sigh. "Now," sharp like a needle into a gum. "Except for the four against, I—"

"Six, six." Dix heard Babe Algol's wheezing screech.

"With apologies to Mister Christel and to Miss Zelta Christel, I am afraid that according to the rules laid down, humanoids are not allowed to partake in a vote of this magnitude." There was a soft, rumbling mumble. "I repeat, except for the four against, the verdict is unanimously agreed."

What's agreed? shrieked Dix. *How did I miss the bloody verdict?*

His other voice shrilled back. *Stop jabbering, you lunkhead, and listen, or else you'll miss something again.*

But that was it—he couldn't hear anything. There was total silence, and all odours had gone with the voices.

Dix came to the conclusion that the times he had spoken to himself took much longer than normal conversation. It seemed to be in a different span of time, perhaps taking longer than even Stuns. This thought made him laugh. *I must be speaking like Stun.*

He remembered Stun, a gaffer sparks in his father's old troupe. "Gov-er-nor." A long pause. "C-an I ha-ve." Another pause. "A wor-d." There was a sharp emphasis on the "d".

Dix imitated Stun's speech pattern, grinning happily to himself as he recalled the man. Stun was one of the most courteous men Dix had ever known, although he didn't look like it. "Serpents would die in fright if they ever saw him," his father would say with a laugh.

Dix vividly remembered Stun's wiry, skinny body and bat-like face, the black and oily skin stretched so tightly that it seemed to force his eyeballs out so that they looked to be on stalks. His mouth had no lips, just crinkled lines that entered his mouth, which one had time to study in great detail because of his slow delivery; when his mouth opened, it revealed gums the colour of burnt cables and a long tongue, black and spliced at the tip in the centre. Whomever he was speaking to knew what he was going to say before he had finished a sentence, but nearly everyone listened politely until he had finished, nodding and smiling and waiting patiently for it to be completed. Luckily, for everyone with whom he came in contact, he had no small talk, and the interchange of words were short and mostly technical.

He was a wizard, a magician with circuitry boards, lighting plots, and routing cables to the myriad of lamps and all the special effects that were used in the extravagant stage shows.

Dix remembered Stun swooping and swinging across the lighting bars high above the stage, from flying gantry to flying gantry, to adjust the position of a lamp by a few degrees or to knock a barn door, metal flaps, to shape the light of the soft-edged Fresnel lens slightly in to shade the beam of light onto or off of a particular area or performer on the stage far below. The slightest, merest touch seemed to transform the whole lighting effect.

If his father was the painter with light, then Stun and his crew of sparks were his brushes that flicked, stroked, and dabbed at the dark, black palette high above the light-painted canvas of the stage, increasing the shadows from the metal, cut-out "Gobos" on the tabs and drapes, teasing out the hues and tones to bring depth and dimension between the wattle and daub, the spark's terminology for the scenery, and the turns for all the performers, no matter how big a marquee name they were.

Dix returned to his problem. *Not only am I speaking slowly, but it obviously cuts out any dialogue or conversation that might be taking place around me like a grave button.* Dix contemplated the grave button, which was used occasionally in rehearsals and only by him, if he was directing from the back of the auditorium when the noise from the technician's technical jargon and the performer's tittle-tattle and gossip had become an overwhelming cacophony. The grave button was an electronic jamming device that killed all other communication systems stone dead, allowing only the director's voice to be heard. It was very effective and gave one an enormous feeling of power and satisfaction.

Sadly, Stun and his sparklets were long gone because of an edict from the all-powerful Corps that theatrical venues would only be allowed a certain kilowatt of power. This edict killed off the extravagant staging of exotic productions but was issued purportedly to conserve the energy of the galaxy. But everyone knew the real reason behind this altruistic sentiment.

Energy was being conserved not for the galaxy, but so that the rich and powerful—once showmen, moguls of the entertainment business who had, by deceit, translated their monopoly of information into political power—could continue their lavish lifestyles as long as possible.

The edict had stated that only a certain amount of electricity could be used in the illumination of stage shows and performances, and the allotment was graded depending on the status of the troupe. All theatre and casino managers were responsible for policing this edict, and most did with enthusiasm and relish, making and applying their own rules and restrictions. If any troupe or theatricals broke these rules and used more of their allocated amount, they were fined, with severe penalties and further restrictions imposed. It was practically impossible for any manager of a troupe to know exactly how many lamps could be used with the allocated wattage, because the casino and theatrical managers would be illegally siphoning off the electricity for their own personal use.

To stop these petty restrictions and fines, most troupes only used one or two vapour-burner spots to follow the acts, and the occasional sodium flare for special effects. The main illumination came from candles supplied by the crematoriums. Stun and his crew became redundant, flickered, and died.

Dix held the mighty and powerful Corps responsible. The energy of the planet hadn't been conserved by switching off a few lamps; it had been transferred to benefit the few and their greedy little empires.

Deepshit bastards, Dix snorted. He had often used this terminology for the people who were in charge of him, who held power over him; it was his way of expressing his frustration at the rules and edicts that were made, often petty and always restricting. It wasn't till now that he had the time to reflect and contemplate. It shocked him because he realized that he was part of the whole system that was helping to preserve the Corps. He had never challenged them, had never stepped out of line, had always carried out their commands, no matter how grudgingly.

He realized now that he was also selfishly protecting his own little empire and himself. *Hucksters, villains, cheating bastards. Look what you have made me into: a simpering toady sycophant, a bum-sucking collaborator.* He felt disgusted with himself.

But what could you have done? said a thought, seeking to apologize.

Dix considered it for a moment. *If I hadn't been so pompous being the grand Dix Dannering showman and impresario . . . Whatever happened, whatever the odds, loyalty to the show came first and the show must go on. If I had given it any thought at all, I should have forgotten all that nonsense of loyalty. I should've thought more about number one, been even more bum-sucking, toadied my arse off, become one of them, joined the inner circle.*

And what good would have that have done? he asked himself.

I could have changed things from the inside, got rid of the bad casino managers.

You? Don't make me laugh. You'd have been swanning about, lapping up the luxury. You wouldn't have given a toss about anyone else.

Dix felt depressed, knowing that this was probably true. Then he brightened up. *Well, it's probably for the best that I'm outside of the tent.*

But you never pissed in, so outside or inside wouldn't have mattered.

No, but perhaps I felt better being an outsider. It didn't give me any conflicts of interests.

His mind drifted back to Stun and his memories of the gorgeously lit stages, the complicated lighting routines that washed across the stage and changed imperceptibly for each mood, from the dramatic to the comedic, and the massive, incredible tableaus that were once staged. He thought of the ambition he used to have. He'd felt that one day he would, perhaps just once, be given the chance of creating one of those exotic, extravagant tableaus, a mind-blowing theatrical event. It was an ambition, a dream that he knew at the bottom of his heart could never ever be achieved.

All the technicians, scenery, clothes, lighting rigs, and lampada had disappeared, probably rotted and rusted away. No theatres or casinos that he had worked in during his lifetime as a producer had retained any of it; few hardly remembered them except for the real old stagers, who even remembered the gorgeous, extravagant productions. The few who did remember were reluctant to talk about them.

He realized how impossible it would be for most people to know that such productions ever existed; even in his own troupe few knew. Xit, Babe Algol, Jollity, and Irma would. The young chorus girls wouldn't. Popablu certainly wouldn't, and Dix doubted he would even care; he was of this time, this era.

It was a sad fact that people today considered the sanitised, utilitarian casinos and theatres the most exotic and the extravagant places they knew.

This was also the cause of the occasional angry outbursts and of demonstrations against these establishments and their extravagant use of precious energy, when more deserving places required it. The demonstrations were quickly and brutally suppressed by the Corp's police force and Sturm Guards. The Corps insisted that all institutions, hospitals, schools, and administration offices in the galaxy had their own power supplies in the form of solar energy and wind power systems that were adequate for their needs.

This had been true many years before, but now these energy providers had ceased to work, and the searing heat of suns had long since penetrated the thinning ozone layers of the planets, evaporating the seas and melting the solar panels. The savage, hurricane winds that swept across the continents had torn down the wind turbines. All the natural energy had been destroyed by the planet's belligerence, once a benevolent host and now a malevolent enemy.

The Corps knew this and chose to ignore it. The few atomic power stations that were still working, still choking the air, and still destroying the ozone were only for the elite members of the planets and the people that helped to protect this status.

Because the existing communication system worked spasmodically and was not reliable for transmitting information, included in this group of people who helped to protect the status were the casino and theatre managers and the people who worked in these venues—which included the various theatrical groups and entertainment troupes. These were allowed to exist because of the sole, cynical reason of propaganda and the relaying of specific information to the inhabitants of the galaxy.

It was through these places and the performers that the Corps could relay its message: "By braving the elements and deprivations that they we are all having to suffer, by all standing together, we shall all finally pull through. Our formidable, brilliant scientists were closing on a formula that would reverse this cosmic Armageddon."

It was a propaganda message. Their formidable brilliant scientists didn't have a clue on how to reverse the Armageddon, and like all the best types of propaganda and misinformation messages, it was subtly released and diffused into songs, dances, and acts that the theatrical companies and touring troupes were given to perform. They could interpret it in any artistic way they wanted; it wasn't a rigid format as long as it stayed on message.

Dix had accepted that he was part of this deception, part of the propaganda machine, and he knew it was the only way of surviving; any dissention, any challenge, any discord would have seen him quickly dismissed and instantly replaced, and he would disappear. So he had chosen to accept it, mitigating his guilt by making his troupe perform at the highest level possible, to give his audiences the very best night out they ever had. He hoped that by achieving this, it might help them escape, for a fraction of a moment in time, from the drudgery and nightmare of their lives. It might help them forget the toxic air that gnawed into the fabric of their homes, or the beige-coloured nights bringing the poisonous, gassy winds shrieking and billowing triumphantly as they scoured the land.

Wonder if I have achieved even that? Dix pondered, and he shrugged doubtfully. *Perhaps a moment or two, I hope.* He shouted out defiantly, *At least I tried!*

Look, his other voice butted in, *if you keep wandering off, you'll miss what is happening. Now, shut up and listen.*

Dix concentrated. There was still silence and no pervading aromas, except for the slightly chemical scent of the sick bay. He stopped concentrating on the silence and drifted into watching the rolling flashing colours. Bruised, purple gashing across fiery sunsets, brilliant reds, bright sparkling whites splashing and rolling over into deep velvet blackness, penetrated and pierced by bouquets of shiny pearl clusters swirling upwards, disappearing and then reappearing like meteorites flashing across the black background that was constantly changing. He tried to retain some of the images and patterns but had no control over them.

If I haven't been conscious, how is it that I can see this amazing transformation of shapes and colours? Where are they from? he mused *I wonder if everyone experiences the same colours and patterns. More likely we all have individual ones unique to ourselves.*

He tried to distinguish the patterns and shapes, trying to see if there was a sequence. He gave up after a while, deciding that they were totally random and letting them dance freely on. He sighed and thought, *That must be a mental sigh, otherwise if it had been physical, it would have registered on the scanners or been noticed by whoever is attending me—Mister Christel, probably, or lovely, beautiful Zelta.* He smiled admiringly. He had almost forgotten that they were humanoids, that they weren't natural human beings, until Popablu had made a point of it. *Sad, really when you think what lies beneath the skin of that perfect body is just wires, chips, speech synthesizes, transponders, and wizards.* Another thought bludgeoned him. *There's probably no one in attendance. Popablu, after having declared that I am clinically departed, would have ordered Mister Christel and Zelta back to their bays.* This made him agitated. *Have I already been jettisoned? Am I already on the way to the great Universal Guignol, my body wrapped in the metallic shroud? Have I arrived?* He had no answer, and he concentrated on the steady hum of the sick bay.

The questions nagged at him again, *Perhaps everyone who is dead isn't, or is physically but not mentally.* A luminous yellow glowed and dissolved into a delicate shade of indigo, but Dix ignored it. *I wonder if the dead can talk to each other?* He whispered, *Hello out there.* he listened for a moment and then shivered, hoping there wouldn't be a reply.

He had always been superstitious, and ghosts and phantoms were included in this irrational fear. Not that he had ever experience the presence of anything—it was simply a feeling that it might be possible for them to exist.

Sometimes when he had been walking alone backstage after a show had finished, to let the adrenalin subside, he had just safety pilot lights flickering in the dark. He had felt that there was someone or something watching him, a presence that never materialised. On those rare occasions when he had had to venture down into the echoing holds of the *Auriga Lick*, although they were silver bright, he was always apprehensive and irrationally frightened, his imagination too fertile.

I wonder if I shout, He plucked up his courage. *Hello, anyone dead out there?* It was a shout, high-pitched and squeaky. He listened tentatively for any reply musing as he did. *I wonder if he's out there listening, old Dad. Haven't thought about him for years.* He sniffed a smile at the faint memory. *Pity he could never remember who my mother was, or said he couldn't.*

"Just chorus, son," his dad would chortle, his large face crumpling. "Could have been any of them—Pixie, Trudy, Apploo, Fyre, Mang, Sty . . ."

"How do you know I'm your son?" Dix interrupted before Dad reeled off all the names of the many girls in the chorus lines he had had.

"No doubt about that, my son." A plate-sized hand slapped Dix on his back. "Born in the proverbial skip just like your old dad."

"That's not incontrovertible proof that you could base your paternity on, is it?"

"Just look at you," his father bellowed, swivelling Dix around to look into a make-up mirror. "No other bugger in the galaxy has our nose." He pushed his face next to Dix's and squinted down his nose before reeling back and roaring with laughter. "That's incontrovertible, my boy, incontrovertible."

And that was that. Dix never questioned it again, accepting that their identical noses were the proof. He also accepted that it was the only proof he was ever going to get in regard to his paternity.

In his early teens he would have liked a DNA test, but he had never dared to ask for fear of risking his father's disapproval, who considered that their identical, enormous protuberances clearly identified their affiliation. It seemed to give his father enormous pride and joy, and whooped with delight when every spot and pimple targeted it—nowhere else, not chin, cheek, or forehead, just his nose. The pimples never seemed to be just normal size; they were always large and pulsating. The nose seemed to cover his whole face, and sometimes he had difficulty seeing round it. He wanted to hide away, to not be seen by anyone. But his father was a showman, and Dix's embarrassing protrusion, with its purulent growths, was never allowed to be an excuse for not performing. He had to go on stage no matter what splotch, blotch, pimple, zit, or carbuncle grew and festered on it. He had pleaded several times to be let off but was never allowed to be.

"On the billings, my son, it says Mandrax Dannering and Son, and that's a contract. Not only a contract with the Corps, who could revoke our licence if you didn't appear, but also with our public who paid hard-earned spondulicks and sacrificed their time to come and see you."

"They haven't come to see me," Dix would mumble.

"Your nose, son, I nose," Dad would say, hooting guffaws at his own joke and giving Dix the habitual slap on his back.

Dix had been too young to rebel; it had seemed to him that the whole troupe had agreed with his father. He didn't realize at the time that they had little choice—none of them dared challenge Mandrax Dannering due to fear of losing their jobs. His nightly purgatory continued to applause and laughter.

"And for your delight and perspicacity, gentle folk, let me introduce to you my son—I have the nose for talent." He tapped his own nose to hoots of laughter from the audience. "My son, a nose by any other name." Dix would be thrust reluctantly on stage by a stage manager and required to stand on his mark in a specially prearranged position, profile to the audience with his chin held high.

"Perhaps you haven't yet identified my son's remarkable talent. Let me highlight and enhance it for you." With a clap of his hands, the theatre was plunged into total blackness, and then a red, pencil-thin, profile laser beam of light swept over the stage and finally stopped on Dix's nose, The beam slightly defocused and refocused, and the nose seemed to be glowing and pulsating.

"There you have it, there you have it," his father yelled, the audience immediately following with their crescendo of applause and laughter. His father waited until it had died away before continuing. "What a gorgeous, fantastic nose that is. What a beauty, isn't it? And no, ladies, you can't take it home tonight." He waited a beat for the titter at this smutty remark to die. "I have had every space navigator in the galaxy wanting to purchase it, but I have always refused. I mean, who would sell their own flesh and blood? Well, not at the prices they were offering." He laughed at his own quip. "And anyway, I don't want my only son and heir left as a hazard light on some crabby old meteorite." The beam would pulsate, giving the effect of a hazard light. "We knows you nose." The pencil-thin beam would snap off, and immediately a spotlight would flick on to his father. "No, this boy is a star in his own right, and we nose it."

In the seconds of darkness, snap-hooks at the end of flying wires were being attached to the leather harness Dix was wearing under his black catsuit.

"We all nose it. A star, ladies and gentlemen." The spot would switch off, and the thin pencil beam of light would shine onto Dix's nose. Instantly Dix would be lifted off the stage and flown high out and over the audience, then pulled along the tracks, spinning back high into the top flies. For the briefest of moments the light would lose him in the blackness, and in that moment, a false nose on a wire would be flown out, a small battery inside it making it glow and sparkle. Then like a meteorite a stream of sparks, and then a ball of fire, would erupt as it streaked high above the heads of the audience, their heads turning en masse to follow its flight. As they did, Dix would be dropped down to the stage, and this was the most frightening moment of the whole act for Dix. The stage hurtled towards him, the counter-weights flying past him, and Dix prayed that they had been checked and rechecked, balanced against his weight. Then a little bounce as his feet touched the deck. As the nose exploded in a shower of sparks at the back of the auditorium, he would be unclipped from the hip harness and be allowed to escape off the stage, running to the dressing rooms and the sanctuary of the costume skips and the dusty, sweaty costumes to hide so that no one would witness him silently sobbing at the humiliation inflicted on him by his father.

The only person who occasionally came to find him was Xit, who would take a large handkerchief from his pocket and gently wipe away his tears, at the same time telling him, "Your dad isn't a bad man. Mad as a rat in a trap, maybe, but not bad. He loves you, in his way, with deep affection, but he is totally besotted with his work, which is paramount to him. The show will always come first with your dad."

"But it's so vulgar," Dix sniffed. "Horribly cheap and nasty."

"That's good."

"No, it's not."

"No, not that the act is good, but that you were critical about it and assessed it."

"You agree, then?"

"Vulgar, cheap, nasty—no. I agree that for you it is humiliating, because you're sensitive about your hooter, but the act itself is clever and gets laughs and applause."

"That's it, then? That's what's it's all about?"

Xit shrugged. "It's what we do." He was soft and friendly, folding the large handkerchief into the shape of an animal's head with large ears. "All we know." The head nodded.

The act and Dix's nightly humiliation finally ended when the false nose, incorrectly primed, whizzed not over the heads of the audience but into the throat of an unfortunate woman, killing her instantly.

It was this tragedy that first made Dix realize how powerful the Galactic Entertainments Corporation was. It was assumed that woman's immediate family would sue his father and the Corp for extreme negligence. This never happened. Powerful lawyers spoke to the grieving relations who, after this meeting, accepted that there was no case to bring, and yes, she had leapt up out her seat immediately after the projectile had been fired, putting herself directly in the path of it. The family accepted the remuneration offered, which couldn't in any way be interpreted as admittance of guilt but as a generous donation from a kind benefactor. Dix remembered that their one plea, which was accepted, was that the death certificate was to read "Accidental death caused by flying theatrical contrivance." They had been allowed to have "nose" dropped from the wording.

It was also about this time when his nose had stopped being a haven for the raging spots and pimples and returned to being practically normal. It was no longer considered extraordinary, and the flying nose act was dropped.

He was never sure whether it was his nose's return to normality that made his father stop using him, or whether Dad had been leaned on by the lawyers. He suspected the latter, knowing that his father would never drop an act that was a crowd puller.

It was also about this time that they stopped performing in the Grand Theatre palaces, and their status as a number one troupe on the number one circuit changed to number three. They had started touring the more salubrious casino venues in the outback of the galaxy, where the deterioration of the planets was more obvious.

Being on the number three circuit had never seemed to dampen his father's energetic enthusiasm, but upon reflection, Dix considered it must have hurt him. But his father would never show it and was always striving to get back to the top again. He never achieved it and had died before his time, everyone said.

Dix, with the help and insistence of Xit, had taken over the troupe, desperately trying to achieve his dad's dying wish. "Get it back up, son. Be number one. You can do it. Chip off the old block," he had wheezed. "They wouldn't hold it against you, being my son."

Dix never achieved it, and he never knew whether it was because he was the son of Mandrax Dannering, or whether it was that he wasn't good enough. He suspected the latter, knowing that he wasn't ruthless enough, knowing that he lacked total conviction, knowing that it took a tremendous amount of balls and total self-belief to be a number one producer. He was good, an okay showman and impresario, but he never had that desperate, cruel determination, ambition, or chutzpah to achieve top billing.

Long ago he had recognized it, had stopped trying or even pretending that his Candle Dancers were any better than they were. He still retained what his dad had called the "variety surprise element" in his troupe, but now it was on a much smaller scale to suit the smaller venues of the casinos. It wasn't anything like the extravagant entertainment of his father's day, by any stretch of imagination.

"A good, strong, sexy chorus line with long legs; a lot of decolletage and big smiles with white choppers. A plus if they can warble, but not a necessity, and they don't have to win beauty contests." His dad grinned. "Always open with them; they give the show energy, then into a short introductory welcome from oneself. Important, that—makes it personal and intimate. Get over to them that you have brought them the best show in the galaxy and that you're proud to be associated with it. Follow that with a broad comedian, fast patter, single liners, one that involves the audience. You're drawing them, in you see. Then bring on a specialist act—magician, escapologist, jugglers. Need lots of oohs and aahs. Give a scene change with a front of tabs act, but keep it quick and simple. Then go into a solo crooner—male, female doesn't matter, but you want romantic, sloppy and nostalgic; it helps the interval sales." His patter was enthusiastic, unstoppable. "You close your first with them and make sure you get them off fast and your house lights up, not full on but just enough for them to see their way to the bar."

Dix listened intently. "Open your second with chorus, raunchy and loud, and then the comic back on for his second spot. Quick burst across from your chorus, then into your second singer, a marquee name, perhaps passed their prime; they come a bit cheaper, but it's a name the audience knows. A known name on your billings gets bums on seats. Get the lardy off with a curtain; you can allow for a bit of adulation in front of the tabs, but you're now into a big mood and set change for your classics. You want a big, roaring out to close on your second.

"Give a longer interval, because you'll have increased the heating just a tad to give them a bit of a thirst. Give them time to get their bums back in their seats." His dad tapped his nose. "Now, they'll be expecting another big opening, but you don't use your chorus or any extravagant wattle and daub. You keep it basic and simple with a solo singer. Curtain that and follow with a folksy comic, stool centre stage in a spot in front of the curtain. You're changing your set for the spectacular tableau. Now chase off the comic with the chorus; they have to explode on with loud music and plenty of timpani, and the girls have to be as raucous as possible to cover the set build. Sky the curtain on a crescendo as loud as possible with lots of action. Whatever the tableau is—your giant turtles, elephants, lions, whatever—you have your waterfalls and fountains, but keep back your pneumatics and pyrotechnics for the finale. Choreograph your acts to do their turns, but never let them upstage the spectacle or the transformation. Get the applause and cheering going, and then drop the curtain or go to black, then up again for your walk down. Don't allow the lardy-dardies more than two or three curtain calls; you don't want your stage crews going into overtime, or it will cost you a packet. Keep your eye on the sly buggers and see that they're not applauding, just to keep the punters at it." He grinned slyly. "Oh, and make sure the turns don't stand about preening themselves. Drop the iron onto them if you have to. You want them in their dressing rooms and out of their clobber, otherwise you'll be hit by the dressers, the frock and fur departments, for more overtime dosh."

Dix had attempted to follow most of this advice, but he had never been able to stage a spectacular tableau. He had once tried to use water effects, but it had been a disaster. The synthetic water hadn't gushed or flowed in streams of pretty, sparkling cascades like real water. It had erupted like a boil being lanced, spewing all over the stage and practically drowning and suffocating the cast and crew. He had never ventured near the spectaculars again.

Babe Algol had been with his father on the number one circuit. Dad had discovered her as a young singer with a voice he liked, and he had promoted her to stardom, where she became a marquee name. She had stayed with him when he dropped down to the number three. He had kept billing her as a star for a long time, even though people started asking who this large, overweight lady was.

Dix had kept her on—another of father's dying requests, and one that he could achieve. However, because of pressure from casino managers for a more popular name, he'd had to drop her down in the billings and apply to the Entertainments Corps for another name. Popablu arrived, and with him Dix's suspicion of him being a spy.

I understand why I assumed it at first, Dix meditated. *But afterwards he never gave me any cause to go on suspecting him. In fact there were several times when he could have reported me but seemingly never did, or I would have been hauled over the coals.* He sniffed. *So I could have been wrong about . . .* He gasped as another memory exploded through him.

Honey and almond blossom—that was the aroma of the women who had been killed by my nose. She had been brought up to the dressing rooms for some reason and laid out. All her family were there, wailing and crying. A little boy clasped onto an old woman, probably his grandmother, and he kept glancing at the woman with the flashing nose impaled in her throat. Then the boy burst in tears and buried his head into the skirts of the old woman. The honey and almond smell lingered in the dressing room days after the body and family had left.

Dix laughed. *Well, that's solved that. Not a spy from the Corps but a spy for the corpse.* His laughing stopped abruptly as a new thought bludgeoned him. *A bloody assassin—that's what he is, out to revenge the killing of his mother, too young to take revenge on my dad.* He gulped. *So he's going to take it out on me.* He gave a gasping squeak. *Going to? He's bloody done it, he's got his revenge—I'm clinically dead. He waited for his chance, and that bastard Docker gave him the opportunity.*

Thoughts swirled around Dix's head. What he couldn't understand was why the others, the most senior—Xit, Babe, Irma, and Jollity— had allowed Popablu to take over. It wasn't in their nature to let a young upstart be in charge of them, even a marquee name. *What's the conniving little toad done, for them to allow it?*

The gentle, sweet aroma of sawn wood broke into the anger and anguish and swept over him, followed by a sharp, tangy smell of sandalwood. A voice whispered. "Mr. Dwix, mwe and the lads mwade you thwis." At first Dix couldn't make out who it was, and then he realized it was Dwolly, the master scene hand. He listened carefully, not wanting any thoughts to cut out what was being said. "Nwot much, I know, but we thought it mwight be a token to twake on your journey."

He thought, *So I am still on the Auriga, not hurtling through space.*

Shut up and listen, another thought commanded.

"We'll mwiss you. You were a gwood gwovenor, one of the bwest. Oh, er, Pwilly came up with mwe, and we decided it was bwest if only two came. Arnum, mwe, and Pwilly were vwoted for. What?" he snapped angrily. "Yes alwight, alwight I've finished."

Dix heard the murmur of another voice. *Pillys, probably,* he thought, *then Dwolly again.*

"We allowed to open it?" he whispered. Another soft murmuring, replied to by Dwolly. "I know he's dead, but this contraption might have swensors." The tangy wood left and the heavy scent of raspberries took over.

"Bugger the sensors," it hissed.

Dix heard the snap of the chromed-levered locks being pulled down, the raspberries growing stronger and more powerful. Then he heard a peculiar squeaking, sucking sound and then Pilly's husky, luscious, sexy voice.

"There, Mr. D. They're from me. The rest of the girls, your freedom queens, all wanted to come and give you one, but as they couldn't, I promised I'd do it for them." The raspberries came close and overwhelming, and there was more sucking and squeaking before it faded away.

"There," Pilly said with a sigh. "Ten of the best kisses in the galaxy, and you look a sight, Mr. D." Sawn wood mixed with the raspberries. "Oy, get your bloody hands off, you little pervert."

"Here, gwive him thwis and let's get out of here—someone's coming." The raspberries and sawn wood mingled and then melted, leaving the tangy sandalwood.

The bouquet of the sandalwood oil materialized into bright yellow, dispersing all the other colours Dix could see. It was beautiful, amazingly clean and pure.

When I'm out of this fucking thing . . . He could see himself banging on the side of the pod. *I'm going to have everything yellow, the whole show—scenery, cloths, costumes, props, make-up.* He decided he'd gone over the top. *With the exception of make-up. It would be sensational, just sensational.* The yellow started to fade. *Don't go, please don't go.*

A dingy, dirty khaki washed over it, bringing with it the sharp, pungent odour of stale urinals. "Fuck you, fuck . . ." Then it stopped as he realized it would be Xit, and he knew he had to concentrate and not drift away. "Old mate, it's Xit. We're getting you out. Know you're alive. Here, grab his legs. Jollity, get his arms." Someone screeched out. "Quietly, for devil's sake," hissed Xit. "Never mind what he looks like, just that daft tart's kisses. Here, Irma, take this bloody thing."

Irma made some comment, but if was to muffled for Dix to understand until Xit replied. "I don't know what it is, some weird fetish that screwball Dwolly made. Sorry, mate, it's going to be a bit . . ." The urinal swooped down. "Rough, and up he comes. Shrite," Xit screamed. "You haven't unplugged him? Do it, do it."

Must be the wires from sensors and respirator that I'm still attached to. Dix knew he was being moved out of the isolation capsule, and he then realized with a jolt that if he was, then Xit and the others were violating one of the strictest rules of all inter-planetary spacecrafts. "No person or persons," he began quoting it, "anthropoid or alien, dead or alive, can be moved from the isolation units without the direct and total authority of the senior medical officer, who, before this authority could be given, would have to have had clearance from the Interplanetary Governing body on health and safety."

In itself the ruling was sound, made to prevent any virus, infections, or malignant or malevolent beings from contaminating or taking control of a spacecraft or space stations. On some ships if the medical decks and shatterproof, glass-domed individual capsules weren't being used for medical reasons, they were deployed as detention centres for criminals, malcontents, and any other beasts, alien or human.

They had never been used for that purpose on the *Auriga Lick*; in fact they were rarely used for medical reasons, and this was why Dix allowed Jollity to use the capsules to propagate and grow his fruits and vegetables; they were ideal because of the air and temperature controls. He had allowed it on the proviso that the whole troupe and crew would share in the produce, which they did. Fresh, mouth-watering fruit and delicious vegetables being delivered to the galley by Jollity with a big grin on his normally doleful face.

Wonder which vegetable or fruit patch I'm in? Dix grinned and then sniffed sadly. *That's what his produce didn't have—any smell, completely odourless.* It was the first time he had realized it.

Smell wasn't what Xit lacked. The soiled underpants leaned into him. "Just going to hoist you up and onto a trolley, Governor. In three. One, two, and over-shrite, the little bugger weighs a bloody ton." Xit gasped. "You all right, Jollity?"

Dix couldn't hear the reply but presumed it had been an affirmative. A splash of burnt alcohol wheezed into the underpants. "Can you manage it between you?"

A grunt was the answer.

"Me and Irma will watch the doors for you, if I can just squeeze . . ." The alcohol slipped away.

Dix visualized Babe Algol squeezing her huge, rolling bulk out of the sick bay. Oh, how he would have loved to physically wallow in her bulk, have her wrap her huge arms round him and smother him between her enormous, wonderful soft boobs. The thought drifted away.

He had no sensation of being moved but guessed by the waves of Xit's foul breath gasping, heaving flatulence mingling occasionally with sweet alcohol and the fragrance of Babe Algol, that he was in transition. *Wonder where they're taking me.*

He heard the occasional whispered words and expletives. "Frigging bloody galley locked. Turn, get him round." The words helped him locate which part of the ship they were travelling through, but he couldn't determine where they were heading. He had made a few guesses to begin with, but they had always been wrong, so he had given up and settled back to enjoy the wafting aromas.

Three

The *Auriga Lick* was a large, sturdy, old ship that looked, as someone once remarked, "like a mound of ancient downy cream coprolite, laced with fairy lights." Most of this class of ships, after being in service for many years, looked the same. Surviving thousands of meteorite storms and solar explosions that burnt the ship's super-structure hard and turned it to a frazzled, dirty ruddy ochre. The innocent-sounding pitter-patter of neutron particles didn't have to be any larger than a grain of sand to cause dents in the hull the size of small craters.

The interior of the *Auriga* was the opposite: clean, burnished, and polished, with every particle of dust sucked and filtered out through the air purifiers.

Dix reflected on the *Auriga* and the first moment he had assumed command, taking over from his father and being given the license to be captain. He had insisted on having the flight deck and his cabin panelled out in rich walnut. It looked fantastic but wasn't real, although it was virtually impossible to tell the difference. The carpenters and scenic artists had reproduced it from a photograph Dix had found of the office of Dulipper Dix Borradox, one of the old-time, great Theatre Palace impresarios. It wasn't that Dix aspired to be like him, or that his father had given him his middle name. He had done it out of nostalgia and in the hope that it might generate some of the magic and spirit of the old days, which might inspire him.

Dix had thought at first that it was his office to which they were heading, but they had veered away and were now heading along the myriad corridors, through the decks and down into the cargo holds.

Dix shuddered involuntarily. The holds were full of illegally held scenery and props from his and his father's shows, which he had secretly hidden away because of the edict issued by the Galactic Entertainment Corporation. The first edict, presented in blue envelopes by theatre and casino managers, had suggested that it would be appreciated if all the variety troupes and theatrical companies were licensed by the Corp. This meant every variety troupe and every theatrical company in the galaxy was under Corps control; no independents survived. They were to devise acts in their shows that stressed the goodness and well-being of the new era and life. No troupe dissented, not wanting to annoy or have a black mark against their name, which would mean they would never be allowed to work again.

A second edict quickly followed, and there was no euphemism concealed in it—this was a straightforward command. It was titled "The Age of Enlightenment".

Bastards, Dix hissed remembering the words of the edict.

No performances are permitted if they have any connection or reference to the decadent past. They are not to have any historical connotations or nostalgic sentiment relating to this past, in any matter or form whatsoever.

Yesterday is forgotten and belongs to the destroyers and polluters of our planets, and we deserve no memory of them. Tomorrow has arrived and belongs to us all.

At first it had been thought that this had meant only the acts and performances, not the props, cloths, scenery, or costumes. It quickly became savagely clear when Sturm Guards, the replacement of the old police force, invaded the Grand Palace Theatres, brutally bludgeoning the managers, performers, and stage crews as they tore down and burnt the scenery, destroying all the props and costumes that had any connection with the decadent yesterdays.

Word spread like the burning gauzes, and instantly all theatre management and casino troupes scrapped and destroyed their scenery, props, costumes, and anything that had any connection with the past.

Rebellious Dix hadn't burnt or scrapped his scenery or props. It was much too precious, held wonderful memories, and was impossible to replace. He and the trusted members of the crew and troupe had secretly hidden it in the *Auriga Lick's* labyrinth of cargo holds. His reasoning had been that it would cost a small fortune to have it all remade, and if sometime in the future there was a more enlightened edict, then he would be ahead of everyone else. This tactic might get him back up to number one.

He was entirely lacking in emotional conviction and knew in his heart of hearts that this would never happen. He knew that he had held onto it not just for sentimental reasons but because it was a small stand of defiance against the sadistic, cynical oppression that was now spawning the new era of show business.

Everything had to be about the rejuvenation of the planets and the galaxy, which was becoming healthy and vigorous and generating new life.

The opposite was true. The cosmos, the galaxy, the great island of stars, and the thirteen inhabited planets were slowly dying, fading, and disintegrating. The planets seemed to have manifested a consciousness, and with it a murderous malevolence, poisoning, and gassing, burning everything that wasn't natural to them, as though they were trying to expunge all foreign matter that was alien to them. It was as though these great stone and rock beasts were trying to cleanse themselves in a last attempt at survival.

It was on these malignant, venomous beasts that the Candle Dancers were ordered to perform the R&PP for the few inhabitants who stoically remained or had little or no choice.

R and bloody PP, snorted Dix. *Reproduction and Propagation Productions.* He started arguing with himself. *And you, with your songs and dances, delivered.*

Didn't have a choice.

You had a bloody choice.

It was what the Corps demanded. Any infringement or opposition would immediately have had my licence revoked, and the troupe would have been disbanded. There could be no appeal.

His mind drifted over the consequences of refusing an order. All names would have been erased from any contract, billings, or books. No member of the disbanded troupe, from the manager down to a number three stagehand, would ever be allowed to work for the Entertainments Corps again. This organization owned and controlled not only the entertainment industry but also all the other industries on all thirteen planets, so the possibility of working ever again was zero.

There were no employment benefits, no benefits of any other kind. He still defended his action. *All terminated when the great and wonderful Corporation took over.*

A decree had been issued, and Dix mentally mimicked the ingratiating tone of it. "It is our policy, in this new age of enlightenment, to give autonomy to the inhabitants of all the planets. They shall have the right and freedom to choose their own destiny, and they will have the right and freedom to escape the fetters of bureaucracy that has restricted and burdened them with petty taxes and tariffs."

The petty tariffs and the petty personal taxes stopped immediately, and all benefits and welfare of any kind ceased, as did the freedom to choose one's own destiny. Working was the only way to survive, and all work was controlled and owned by the Corporation.

The entertainment industry was booming unlike the majority of other industries, which were in decline, with thousands of workers laid off. The bloated bellies of starvation littered the planets.

Entertainers were used to take the population's minds away from this fact. There was no opposition to the edict; R&PP was enthusiastically embraced, and the audiences loved it.

Dix had been amazed that the old theatrical adage, "Never overestimate the intelligence of your audience", was actually true. But he wanted and felt he had to be more imaginative with his productions, rather than just putting on sex shows like the other casino troupes, with everyone prancing about naked, simulating copulation and fornication for the whole of the performance. No, he wanted to be more inventive, more subtle.

It was also a sad fact that his Candle Dancers were more mature than the other troupes, and their physiques didn't lend themselves to bouncing about stark naked. In all probability, Dix had concluded, it would have put audiences off reproduction and propagation forever. He had therefore decided that sexual innuendo was a much more powerful, suggestive message than blatant sex acts.

Xit and Babe Algol were the only two who resisted at first. "Not for any of your moral or puritanical reasons," they had argued. "Just look at us—our bodies, our physique wouldn't look to good in any kind of sexual display." Babe had added quietly, "Sadly."

Dix agreed wholeheartedly, especially in regard to Xit. Even he couldn't devise or create an act that would make him sexy and give him any sex appeal. No, reproduction and propagation was dead as far as Xit was concerned.

They had both come up with the idea that Xit would go on stage and shout abuse at the audience using every expletive he knew, which was an astounding amount. Even words that weren't expletives—normal, everyday words—Xit could use them and make them sound vulgar. On the first nail-biting tryout, with Dix at the prompt corner in a cold sweat, the packed house jeered and hurled insults back at him, enjoying every moment. When Xit finally limped off, they cheered and applauded him. It was as if they needed it to express their own frustration, their own throbbing anger. His act was a success and in popular demand.

Babe Algol was different. Dix had disliked what he had been forced to ask her to do. He disliked having to choreograph and direct her performance, which he considered extremely shocking and salacious and embarrassing.

The first time she had stepped on stage, he had felt hurt and degraded and could hardly watch.

However, after the first moment, after the first veil had been theatrically whisked away, she had been delighted and overwhelmed by the audience's reaction, when applause and appreciation had thundered out.

Apart from her very suggestive dancing, what she appreciated even more was that they had responded to her voice. Her voice still held the cadence of a young girl but was now rich and sonorous, so apposite with the massive, heaving bosom and the swathes of pink flesh that rolled and shook from her curly, frizzed head to her black satin shoes.

She became a star overnight, hailed as sensuously beautiful, the paragon of sexuality, and (the most hurtful for Dix) the fertility symbol and embodiment of the Reproduction and Procreation program.

He had felt even more hurt and demeaned when he had been ordered to use a picture of Babe Algol, posed in the most lewd and salacious position, for all his publicity material. Dix had never been able to rationalize his feelings about Babe Algol.

Once he had nearly killed Jollity, who had expressed that if he wasn't totally besotted with Irma, he would love to have sex with Babe. After Dix's hands had been pulled off the thin, scrawny neck, both sat recovering, Dix from his bloated eyes and pulsating anger and Jollity from being shaken and thrashed around the back of the stage like the knob end of a rope. Dix had insisted that Jollity needed instant psychiatric help or, at the very least, to have his eyes tested. Whether Jollity ever did either was open to question; he certainly never again expressed any sexual desires about Babe, and whenever he was near Dix, he always popped on a pair of spectacles.

Xit was asked numerous times by the troupe why Dix reacted so irrationally in regard to Babe, and why was he so protective of her. Xit insisted he didn't know, but few were convinced and continued to ask him why no one was allowed to openly criticize her and why any slightly derogative remark made in his presence prompted an immediate retraction or apology. Had there been a romantic tryst in the past? Was it jealousy that made him react like he did? Xit could only shake his head and insist he didn't know anything.

There was certainly no romance suspected now. Babe would practically ignore Dix and sweep by him as though he didn't exist, never acknowledging his presence. Of course, like any professional, she accepted his notes and direction, but she never looked at him, holding her head high and her yellow, goat-like eyes focused above his head onto a spot in the distance, her whole body held still and solid. She would wait until he had finished speaking, until he had backed away with his head lowered with a gracious, reverential smile on his lips, before she would finally unfreeze and move jauntily away.

Dix gulped. *She must care for me.* Her aroma drifted past him, and he mentally squeezed his eyes close to hold back the tears he felt rising up. He had been elated that Babe had deigned to assist in his escape. *After all these years, she's finally showed she cares.*

The stench of cheese pervaded and changed the direction of sentiments. *Two decks below. Must be in the cargo holds, the one with the scenic cloths, gauzes, and cheese.*

Not cheese.

Knew it wasn't cheese, he said sulkily. *Knew it had to be the white primer used for coating the canvas cloths before they were painted. He* imagined them on their specially designed wracks stacked high above him like the furled sails of an ancient galleon, each one carefully rolled on the wooden bars and never folded because that would crack the paint.

"There must be . . ." He attempted to visualize them, to remember how many they could have stored in the hold. "Hundreds." He gave up trying to mentally count them. "All of them masterpieces in their own right."

His memory selected a scenic cloth that had been his favourite. He had been enchanted by it, rushing into the auditorium to watch it being unfurled. Even before it was stretched out taut, even before it had been lit, it was amazing. And then when Stun and his crew of sparks played and painted it with light, the marvellous, magnificent magic of this two-dimensional painting leapt out, transformed into three-dimensional reality.

Dix visualized it again. The tall, porcelain white columns towering up into the clouds, their flutes and cornices glowing with sunlight that also picked out the intricate lattice woodwork of the framed arches interlaced with orange and white climbing roses. Dix had felt that he could dance through them and round the columns, crossing the glass floor. Below flowed a lapis lazuli stream curving to the large, open windows through which a landscaped garden could be seen with rich with topiary hedges and trees of every description dripping with fruit or covered in brightly coloured blossoms.

Sad, Dix lamented. *Probably no one will ever see it again; perhaps it has even perished, rotted away.* He chided himself. *I should have taken more care of them.* He answered defensively, *There never seemed to be enough time.*

He knew that this was an excuse and that he could have made time. That is, if he hadn't been terrified and scared of being found out, found guilty of hoarding memorabilia from the decadent past. As he had grown older, he had tried to forget about the scenery, never venturing near the holds if he could avoid it. He use to have nightmares that the Sturm Guards had discovered it, and he was being paraded on stage, naked and spotlit and denounced as a yesterday man.

The cheese died, pounced on by Xit's putrid breath. "Nearly there, Governor. Hang on a bit longer; only got to cross the gun decks, and we'll be there."

Four

*T*he gun decks exploded into him, not from the acrid stench of sparking electrical circuits or smouldering transistors like most gun decks. No, this was the *Auriga Lick*, and her gun decks smelt of lacquered wood.

What a long time ago that was, Dix thought with a chuckle. *That communiqué, ordering the refit of the lower decks to carry cannons.* He breathed in the aroma of lacquered wood. *It was before the Entertainment Corporation took over, a long time before, before they annihilated any opposition by their conniving deceit.*

He contemplated the past. Wars were always erupting between the thirteen inhabited planets, but a particular war, the Final War, the War to End All Wars, was the reason for the refit to be ordered. Younios, the sixth planet, was ruled by a belligerent junta called the Tuns, who had decided they wanted to expand their space and had attacked and laid siege to the planet Ghlossa of Mayios.

Seven of the other planets—exhausted by their own long-drawn-out wars, incessant fighting, and the futile and endless succession of bloody battles, massacres, and rapes followed by pestilence, famine, and decimation of the populations—decided to join forces to protect Ghlossa of Mayios. A decision was made and an order announced: all the ships belonging to the Seven Comity of Nations were to be armed and prepared for battle. This included civilian, merchant and Auriga-class ships.

Dix and his Candle Dancers were travelling towards Martios Velona, one of the smallest, poorest, and most barren of the planets, when they received the order. They were a long, long way from the war zone and the aggressive Tuns.

I suppose that's one good thing since they took over, Dix mused about GEC. *No more wars.* This thought amazed him. *No more of those awful bloody wars.*

Then he quickly qualified it, not wanting to give them any credit. *Bastards. Perhaps the wars were the best time of our lives. We were free, and it certainly brought us together and united us against the others. Not like now, when you can hardly trust anyone and are suspicious of everything and everyone. Wary and cautious, judging every situation and conversation before replying or reacting, just in case you are being spied on or they are trying to entrap you.* He nodded sagely. *So you keep yourself to yourself, never expressing your inner thoughts, not even to your nearest and dearest friend. Well, except when you're pissed.*

That's what you did with Docker, tried to entrap him, his other voice said. *Or at least, tried to do.*

Did what, did what? he shouted defensively, listening immediately for a reply. When there wasn't a response, he sulked. *That was different, and anyway, I was not being underhand—that was a genuine, innocent situation that I had not engineered.*

No, but you took advantage of it, his thoughts snapped back accusingly. *In the old days, you would have told him to bugger off. That would have been honest and upright. Now you're just as bad as them—even worse, because you pretend, in your sanctimonious way, that you're not like them. Bloody lucky he killed you.*

Just a minute, just a minute, he said before the voice faded. *Killed me? Not sodding dead yet. And lucky?* He tried to raise his hands. *You call this lucky?*

Truly lucky, because if he hadn't knocked the seven stages of shit out of you, and you had been allowed to rat on him, then you would have been just like them, an unscrupulous and opportunist toad.

Dix considered it for a moment, some part of his mind offering a flood of denials and excuses. Then he quietly replied, *Tell me what other options I had.* He knew his answer was cowardly, was morally shit. *I've got to use their ways, their methods, if I am—if we are to survive.* There was no reply.

Xit's breath pierced his personal argument. "Having a breather. You're no lightweight to haul about." The sharp, pungent ordure receded and was replaced by the soft, fuggy smell of rubberized flooring.

The gun deck, Dix said knowingly, and he wanted to ask Xit if the black neutron cannons were still there, still in their tiers, still gleaming and polished, still with their pretend echolocation missiles. *No, probably not,* he replied to his own question. *Probably covered in layers of dust if the ventilation system had been closed down.* He couldn't remember if it had or hadn't, although he was supposed to have been in charge of things like that. He had been in charge of many things, and the gun decks were his total responsibility.

"Man the cannons," he remembered shouting after the carpenters and painters had finished their work. Dix had designated himself master and commander, and his command post was in the semicircular communication consul that held the camera's monitors in the centre of the gun decks. It was the beginning of the rehearsals for action stations. Everyone was there, cast and crew, and each had been given a part to perform. A rough outline of a script had been written, although a certain amount of improvisation was to be allowed. "Man the cannons!"

He had loved it as the crews raced across to their stations by the cannons and yelled, "Cannon Marigold loaded and locked, sir." "Cannon Tulip loaded and locked, sir." The cries of the crews sung out around him, each cannon given the name of a flower, a beautiful bouquet, a wreath of lethal firepower—if they had been real!

"All cannons locked and loaded, sir."

"And are you ready?" he would call back to the deck commanders, who usually looked up to the cameras above them and held their thumbs up to signal affirmative. Occasionally to add drama to the exercise, one of the gun crews would pretend that their cannon had a malfunction.

Dix would order a maintenance crew "on the double" to sort out the problem, and soon the drama queens would yell out, "Cannon battle—worthy, sir. Request permission to return to command station."

"Permission granted," Dix would yell back, spinning round 360 degrees in his chair before issuing his next order. "All gun crews stand alert. First cannons commence firing. Second cannons commence firing. Third cannons commence firing . . ."

All cannon commanders, on being given the order, would begin to mimic the sound of the firing cannons. "Da, da, da, da . . . boosh, boosh, boosh . . . whow, whow, whow."

The crews swivelled about left, right, up, and down, all pretending to aim their cannons at an attacking force. Smoke bombs and pellets, flashing sparks, pyrotechnics, and dry ice poured into the area gave it an authentic feeling, or what Dix considered actual reality. Lrac and Sivad, the musicians, under-scored the action with shimmering, rousing percussion.

Everyone, including Dix, thoroughly enjoyed playing on the gun decks, acting out heroic actions, and being killed in the most spectacular, dramatic fashion—or a favourite enjoyed by all of them, being mortally wounded, held in someone's arms, and sympathetically caressed by a nurse (chorus girl) till their last dying moment, gasping out their last dying wish in the most hammy, over-the-top acting.

It was amazing, Dix meditated. Although we enjoyed playing the roles, we all took it so seriously. He smiled and felt proud. *If you hadn't known that the cannons were replicas, just wood painted with black shellac varnish, and the explosions and sparks were coming from them were special effects, you wouldn't have known them from the real thing.*

He felt the cold, clammy feeling again as he remembered what he had done, still amazed he'd had the gall to do it. *I was young and didn't think of the consequences,* he excused himself. *Wouldn't do it now, wouldn't dare do it now. Then, I suppose I didn't give it much thought.*

He had simply diverted the money, issued to him by the Ministry of War for the installation of gun decks and to purchase cannons, to a much worthier cause. The wooden cannons and the plywood cladding, painted to resemble the metal covering of a gun deck, had cost him a fraction of what it would have cost to install the real thing. It had allowed him to totally refurbish the scenery and costumes, mostly from his father's time, that were old and falling apart. There was also a tidy sum left over which he had decided to keep for a rainy day.

Unfortunately the rain arrived quicker than he had expected.

Dix had received a direct command that the *Auriga Lick* was to proceed with extreme haste to the battle front. "Grid reference to be adhered to with no deviation."

Given that I had thought, obviously . . .

He remembered the words he had rehearsed when the time came for him to explain to the crew the slightly awkward situation in which they found themselves. "Well, as you all know the money allocated by the Ministry of War for the purchasing of weapons, cannons, et cetera was not used for this prescribed, authorized usage." He breathed in deeply. "It was used, as you all know, in part to make a facsimile, an exact reproduction of a gun deck, and in particular for refurbishing the scenery and costumes that we hold in storage." He had paused and then said hesitantly, "It never occurred to me that we mere thespians, mere song and dance artists, members and crew of the *Auriga Lick*, would ever see or be engaged in any aggressive action, would ever be called, would ever have to do any fighting." He closed his eyes. "We didn't expect we'd ever have to go to war." He licked his lips nervously and opened his eyes. "Or that anyone in his right mind would ever consider using us in such a way."

He gave a significant pause before continuing. "Well, unfortunately I have received a communiqué ordering us to proceed with extreme haste to the battle front, and there isn't any way of avoiding it." He would look at them, eyeball them. "It has been a shock."

Shock was an understatement. Every ounce of blood had left his face, every single hair on his head and from his entire body had instantly turned yellowish and then had fallen out, never ever to grow again. He had retched and vomited with despair, and his skin had ripened to the dusky, blotched green of old age. Dix could still sense in part of his mind the cold, clammy, frozen-jaw, gagging throat feeling when had first decoded and read the signal from the war Ministry.

Rules of Engagement

Younios the sixth planet, and the nominated space of this said planet, is the designated theatre of war. All spacecraft in the Auriga class are to proceed with extreme haste to this theatre. There can be no refusal or avoidance—this is red priority. The junta now controlling the planet Younios has declared war on the planet Ghlossa of Mayios. This belligerent act of aggression has been condemned by all the twelve nations. All Aurigas are required to be vigilant and battle ready. All ships bearing the Tun insignia are to be immediately engaged and fired on. No surrender is to be accepted and no prisoners taken. The nation of Tuns is to be eradicated and exterminated with extreme prejudice, without qualification or vindication. This is total and absolute declaration of war.

It was signed and counter-signed by every general, space marshal, and war cabinet minister on all the planets.

After reading it and rereading it, and after hours of nail biting and gut-churning deliberation, Dix finally reached a decision on what his action would be.

"I have recently received a communiqué from the high command of the war ministry," he said as calmly as he could to all the members of crew that had assembled on the imitation gun decks. He hoped the high-pitched squeak in his voice would be thought to be excitement rather than fear. The decision he had reached was to tell them the truth.

He fought back the nausea that was welling up inside him and banged his fists on the console for quiet. He waited patiently for the babble of voices to stop and allowed a moment of silence for all eyes to concentrate on him before beginning. "The Tun Junta of the planet Younios, who have been waging war on the planet Ghlossa of Mayios, have finally and victoriously been vanquished and defeated by the collective might of the twelve nations, and we . . ." He took a deep, gasping breath, having rattled out the first words. He blinked in amazement that he could hardly believe what he had done, that virtually in the same moment that he had started to speak, he had changed his mind about telling them the truth. The casualty of war was the truth. He continued. "We are requested to take part in the victory celebrations—a great, great honour."

Even now, with fug of the gun deck pervading his senses, he could feel the churning of his stomach when he had stood in front of the whole cast and crew and had blatantly lied. *I suppose I've always been a liar.* The flickering thought flashed. *Perhaps it goes with the job?* He grinned, visualizing the job interview.

"And what position have you applied for?" said a pompous voice.

"Err, producer," he replied.

"Qualifications?"

"Err, liar."

"Excellent. Start immediately."

Obscure laughter, followed by his shadow's voice, which was full of contempt. *You are one of the most contemptuous types of liars, the liar who tells a lie and then convinces himself that it is the truth.*

If required, yes, Dix answered weakly.

Listen to yourself. The voice sneered and began repeating Dix's dialogue with the *Auriga's* crew after his first lie to them.

"It is an honour and a privilege that may allow us the opportunity and possibility of moving from of the number three circuit up to number two and, dare I even say it, back to number one."

The voice said derisively, *You couldn't resist embellishing it, could you?*

Dix wasn't listening; he was listening again to the murmur of surprise and then the whooping of laughter and the thunderous applause, seeing the happiness in all their faces and the way they looked at him in total admiration, as though it had been he who had honoured them and not the Ministry of War. Then after realizing that it had been him, he felt the pounding pangs of guilt.

But only for a brief moment, because now he wanted fervently to believe in it, to believe the lie and nurture it. He had grasped at an idea that had squirmed into his head, and there was a possibility of making it come true.

If I delay as much as possible in getting to Younios, he remembered thinking to himself, *then there is a chance—a good chance, given the odds, twelve against one—that this must result in total victory. It has to be.* He had totally convinced himself that the Tuns were a loser and that there could be only one possible outcome. He obstinately nurtured the illusion, becoming quite jubilant and loving the adulation; he was happy to join in the celebrations that followed.

This hadn't helped his hair to start growing again, or his skin to recover from the greenish white colour of poisonous mistletoe berries. Neither did it stop the cold, clammy sweats.

The feeling did not stop when their ship was on the delaying tactic, still orbiting the coiled rope stratosphere of Martios Velona. And when no one had been detailed to be on watch or vigilant. And when, after yet another night of jubilant celebration, an excessive amount of liquid refreshment had been consumed and everyone had retired to their cabins and beds. And then all the lights, except for the emergency signs, had been switched off, including the surveillance cameras. At that time a squadron of the Tun, armed and primed for battle and on their way to annex the small, barren planet of Martios Velona—after annexing the Ghlossa of Mayios by conquering and defeating the twelve nation states in a ferocious battle won against incredible odds that would go down in annals of history. The feeling did not stop when this squadron of the Tun surrounded and engaged the *Auriga Lick* in battle.

Dix could still remember the enormous gulp he had swallowed when he had been informed that five battleships were slowly circling them—five battleships all with the blood-red Tun insignia emblazoned on their sides. Five battleships, each one several times larger than the *Auriga Lick*, all bristling with guns like sea urchins, each spike a Chameleon cannon.

"Surrender!" Dix had screeched, making his hangover throb even more. "Surrender!" he had sobbed, racing onto the gun decks to switch on every microphone, every camera, every screen to open up a communications signal. "We surrender!" he cried out as he watched on the visual display screens all five Tun battleships lift the huge, curved plates that covered their cannons like basilisk lizards opening their eyes. They sighted and aligned on the small *Auriga Lick*. "Surrender!" he shrieked out at the top of his voice, praying there would be a response and also praying that they hadn't intercepted the communiqué from his high command.

He squealed out in stomach-turning terror, clasping his hands across his mouth and shaking from head to toe.

"Tell them we're actors," someone had hissed hysterically in his ear, at the same time pulling at his hands. "Tell them, tell them—thespians, not combatants . . ."

This plea had been interrupted by the mimicking whine of one of their own cannons being fired. Their own wooden cannons. "Da-da-da . . . twoosh-twoosh-twoosh." Dix spun around, galvanized into action by utter disbelief, to find out who was committing such a suicidal action. "Get that fat arse off that cannon!" he screeched seeing the dark silhouette of a figure shaking as if firing.

The figure was quickly wrestled and dragged off the cannon, and it seemed that in that same moment of time, before Dix could even squeal out another "Surrender", a single collective gasp from everyone on the *Auriga Lick* had sucked in every murmur, every squeak, every breath, leaving a silence that was weightless and deadening. In that collective, singular moment, the five gashed, battle-scarred, dark green battleships fired, unleashing a soundless crackle, a flickering, flashing, splash of raging, roaring, eye-searing red waves that swept towards the *Auriga Lick*. Perhaps in that split nanosecond, everyone on board experienced the moment before inevitable death.

In that one-billionth of a second flick of an eyelid, the five battleships' spat out shimmering, bright, flame-red rods that hit every side, every orifice of the *Auriga Lick*. Then every actor, dancer, singer, comedian, stagehand, rigger, painter, stage manager, electrician, dresser, musician, producer died.

Some remembered Dix grinning to himself and had died quite dramatically, collapsing and writhing on the floor or clasping their hearts and sinking slowly to their knees, heads tilted back with beatific smiles on their faces. Some had just blinked, and others closed their eyes and lowered their heads.

But then there was a bewildered wariness, when they all realized that they were still alive and were not dead. Stuttering snorts of laughter and puzzled heads were shaken, and then the realization that they had experienced a kind of miracle.

It wasn't the miracle of being alive. The miracle they had experienced came from the five battle-scarred ships bearing the Tun insignia on their sides. And it wasn't the loud, collective bellow of laughter from these five ships that had boomed through the open communication channels immediately after the salvo of the flame-red rods had hit the *Auriga Lick* with a reverberating clonk, even though this in itself was a minor miracle because the Tuns had never been heard or known to laugh.

The miracle was that the Tuns—the most despised, the most feared, the most bloodthirsty, the most hostile and belligerent inhabitants of the galaxy, and the ones who were said to be totally devoid of humour and had no faculty of perceiving what was amusing or comic—had actually and certainly cracked a joke, and the *Auriga Lick* was the butt of it.

A fraction of a second after the bellowing laughter, and in the reverberating echo of it, the terrible, despicable Tuns had gone, leaving the *Auriga Lick* spinning round in a small, black whirlpool of space. She was still intact, and except for the flame-red rods sticking out of her outer skin and making her look like a blushing hedgehog, no damage had been caused.

All the dead on board had breathed a collective sigh. The ones who had died dramatically raised themselves up onto their elbows, smiled, and shrugged, slightly embarrassed. Others laughed and whooped, unable to believe that they were still alive after the close encounter with the dreaded Tuns.

When a closer inspection had been made of the rods, they were found to be long, slender dowels of wood sprayed with phosphorescent paint. Everyone was slightly puzzled and bemused before realizing that the fierce, warring Tuns had fired the wooden dowels at the *Auriga Lick's* wooden cannons.

Even now, Dix was amused by it. It had been a miracle, a remarkable miracle that to this day he couldn't understand why they hadn't been blasted into oblivion. He had been thankful of the Tun's humour, thankful that there was no harm done to his crew.

"Get that fat arse off there." He heard his own voice screaming again.

Why did that screech back into my mind? he wondered. He tried to recall who it was he had screamed at, who the fat arse had been.

He felt a pang of pain, felt the salty tears curling down his face and into the corners of his mouth, felt incredible sadness. But he couldn't recall who it was or why he felt like this. *Shrite, if I could ask Xit, he would know.*

The pages of his memory slowly began to turn, and pictures emerged onto the white sheets. At first a shock of cream hair faded in, and then a round red face pierced with large, bright blue, twinkling eyes. Then a lop-sided mouth that was quick to smile.

Prinders! laughed Dix. *Shry Prinders. What a lovely man.*

He could see this small, dapper, fat man, once the choreographer of the show, dancing in front of him and explaining a new set of steps for a dance routine in his slightly lisping voice. "Side together, cross over, spin round, shoulder role, dip down, arms thrown back, and behind with thumbs touching to pull the scapulars together, thrusting out the mammaries. Yes, Mr. Dix, worth the shoe leather?" He had been very reserved and would avoid using any common words for bodily parts; arse would be derriere.

"Yes, Mr. Prinders, worth the shoe leather."

The picture also recalled why Dix felt so sad. Shry Prinders was the one and only casualty in the battle with the Tuns. He had not realized that the *Auriga Lick* was engaged in a real situation. He had heard the rattle of footsteps outside his cabin and realized they were all running towards the gun decks, and he had immediately assumed it was another rehearsal. He had quickly dressed in his combat gear and had run as fast as he could to get into position. Upon thinking he was late, he had immediately started firing.

Unfortunately, when he had been wrestled off his cannon, the smallest splinter of wood had pierced his chin. He hadn't paid much attention to it at the time because there were much more dramatic events taking place. But the splinter had a small amount of phosphorus impregnated in it, and a few days later he had painfully died.

It was unfortunate, Dix sniffed. *Sad that he didn't have a medical . . . Suppose you wouldn't, for a little splinter. Still pretty wretched that no one, not even me, wondered where he was for three days, and then when we discovered him in his cabin, it was too late.* Dix shuddered, wishing now that he hadn't recalled Shry Prinders and knowing now why he had been blocked it from his memory, why he had attempted to erase it.

As the cabin door was axed open, everyone had reeled back, intuitively covering their mouths and noses from the putrefying stench that blasted out at them. After recovering, the bravest, clasping shirts or jackets over their heads, had entered but only for a moment. They were quickly repulsed, retching and vomiting after seeing the face of Prinders. The skin round his mouth had peeled away, leaving a festering jaw bone and teeth. His quick smile was fixed into a permanent grin, and his twinkling blue eyes had dissolved into dusty gray spots. He was still alive—the bubbles erupting through the holes that were once flaring nostrils certified that. Mister Christel was called to examine Prinders and had diagnosed phossy jaw, a particular virulent gangrene that fed on decomposing tissue, probably caused by the small splinter he found embedded in the skin that had been the jaw.

"If it had been treated in the early stages it could have been arrested." Mister Christel had given a significant pause. "But now he will die slowly and painfully, even if I administer every pain-killing drug at my disposal. Unless . . . ?"

Dix had instantly known what the "unless" had meant. But was he brave enough, man enough to make that decision?

The memory was renewed: his agony; the sudden and irrational hatred of Prinders, who had put him in this position; then instantly forgiving him, his heart aching love of him; and then knowing that the moment he had heard "unless", he knew what his decision would be. He knew that his love for the fussy little man—who loved his work, who was a tyrant with his girls until they had his steps to perfection, who would then shower them with presents and praise—would make the decision for him.

That was one of the most awful decisions I have ever had to make in my whole life. He remembered the moment in vivid detail.

"Yes, Mister Christel, at once." Tears had filled his eyes, and his heart felt as though it was being strangled.

The injection was given instantly.

"Mr. Shry Prinders, killed in action while defending the *Auriga Lick*," was the inscription on the silver shroud wrapped round the body inside a space pod, launched after a burial ceremony where everyone was weeping.

Dix swallowed hard, fighting back the tears that were welling up again. He was also praying that Mister Christel's pronouncement that Shry Prinders had passed away immediately after he had administered the lethal injection was correct. *And not like it is with me.*

Xit's searing breath lacerated and erased the memories. "And off we go again."

Perhaps this is the final stage, Dix thought, attempting again to work out where the final destination would be.

Five

ravelling downwards, he thought as he sniffed. *Into the bowels of the* Auriga. The faint aroma of lubricating oil and the monotonous murmuring of the gravitation gyroscopes convinced him this was where they were heading.

He had only been to this level twice before. Once was when he was very young, taken there by his father who had thought it extremely important that every member of his troupe had some knowledge of the mechanical and electrical magnetic elements of the ship, from the fluttering electron pulses to the mercury soil tanks.

The second time was a few years ago, when one of the chorus line—he couldn't remember her name, a flamenco dancer who was tall with black hair, not unlike Irma—had gorily committed suicide. A reason was never found; he had always suspected it had something to do with Popablu but had never probed, never investigated it, in case it revealed a cesspit connected to him.

Dix visualized the myriad intestinal bulwarks and the labyrinthine, curved corridors with walls of burnished metallic foil, the floors underlit by white incandescent fluorescent cubes that led to the recycling, sewage, and fusion plants, isolating the vast neutron fuel tanks and the powerful gyro-magnet.

A sanitized streaky white and silver maze, taking and reflecting the colour of whoever or whatever was in it. It was a place where one could get totally disoriented and lost for days, only being found when the heat and kinetic sensors were checked to establish that no alien life forms had arrived on board. This scan was very rarely done, and the sensor's warning sirens had been disconnected nearly instantly after they were installed; they were much too sensitive, shrieking out at the merest fleck or particle of dust that happened to be floating round. The practice of checking them at all had also ceased, partly because the robotic maintenance sentinels were now totally relied on, partly out of sheer laziness, and partly because no one ever ventured down there. But mostly it was because no new alien life forms had been discovered in the galaxy for many years now. What alien life forms there had been, had been integrated, into society years before if benevolent; if malevolent, then they had been exterminated.

Interplanetary space travel was no fun anymore, Dix quipped. *Nothing to laugh at all. No malevolent alien fiends preying on space travellers.* He remembered the old navigators' and pathfinders' yarns about these creatures and monsters after their expeditions to the outer limits of the great islands of stars and uninhabited planets in the spiral arms and vast, silent, dark deserts of the galaxy. There were clusters of shiny, black-scaled Ptero-octopods that could envelop largest of ships, sucking out every member of the crew to leave an empty shell in which they could breed and house their pupae.

In fact, not much to laugh at all. Sounds like one of Jollity's lines.

Then his flippancy changed into melancholy. *The galaxy should be the best and safest place to be. Perhaps it had been once, before it was polluted and poisoned, every food chain contaminated in the aggressive drive to achieve the maximum profit.*

His moroseness filtered away as he wondered why Xit was taking him into the bowels of the *Auriga Lick,* and he attempted to rationalize it. *Perhaps he's found an area where I can be totally hidden, completely safe from Popablu's searching.* He knew the search would be inevitable, and he started to speculate on what Xit intended to do. *There are no life support systems down here, only the maintenance sentinels crawling along to check the rivets, seams, air locks, and jettison tubes.*

Dix shivered and felt suddenly cold with his next thought. *Perhaps he has a plan on how to revive me.* Then he felt even colder. *Resurrect me, bring me back into the land of the living. Perhaps he's thinking of performing some kind of medical operation.* He shook his head, trying to rid himself of this line of thinking and desperately hoping it wasn't anything to do with operations and revival techniques used in the past decades. He'd heard tales of how people were reduced somehow to anti-matter and then rejuvenated. *Total comic book fantasy, folklore that has no scientific basis to it.* He shouted out, trying to communicate his fears with Xit. Then another thought oscillated into his mind. *Perhaps like most of the old folklore tales, this might have substance of reality bedded in it.* He grappled with this proposition. *Perhaps people had been brought back from the dead—not in the way of the old tales, but perhaps in the days when medicine was still in its very primitive stages, when surgeons still used knifes and scalpels to peel back skin to find life, or lasers to burn through flesh. Back when computers still had wires and circuit boards, and when it was certainly impossible to tell for absolute certainty that one was dead. Then, yes . . . yes, it could have been possible to resurrect, or to have seemed to do so, if most probably they weren't dead in the first place.*

His imagination suddenly and inexplicably flashed to a grotesque image of Babe Algol, clad in white plastic surgical apparel and advancing towards him while clutching a squirming, flesh-pink reptile, intent on thrusting it into his mouth. "Just a spoonful, come on, there, open wide," she simpered, waving the thing at him.

"No, Miss Algol, please no." He defended himself as best as he could by clamping his mouth tightly and shaking his head from side to side, as he had done when he was a small child and any horrible medicine or pills were being administered, continuing this action until they were eventually taken away. It still proved to be an effective performance, and the image of Babe Algol faded away. He felt himself perspiring and was amazed that this memory of Babe Algol had surfaced, and that it always seemed to be her that was attempting to administer him the spoonfuls of medicines or handfuls of pills, just like any mother would do.

He wasn't allowed to meditate on this as another thought jostled it away. *It is quite probable, from my current predicament and my observation of it, that when I was in the medical unit, the bright blue electronic words on the computer, with its super-sensitive, diagnostic powers, scrolled through, having analysed every individual and macroscopic part of my anatomy, including every tissue and the cells of my brain, giving negative responses to them all and then flashing its final analysis.*

"Nervous system totally devoid of sensitivity. Brain cells unresponsive and non-regenerative. Life form extinct." This might not be true and was therefore no more reliable or infallible than the old methods and the old computers.

He reflected on this for a moment. *I am thinking, and therefore I am,* he said smugly, and then he added, *Xit just might be onto something.*

He let his breath out very slowly and ruminated. *Xit, having never shown any knowledge, interest, or expertise in anything medical—except his ability to change his catheter bag—is possibly now going to perform some kind of operation that would result in me being brought back from the dead, a resurrection.*

It didn't fill him with confidence. *But perhaps, who knows. I was ascertained dead by a computer.* A despondent shrug was his only rational comment, having no choice but to accept whatever the outcome was going to be. They were probably now close to the sewage and fusion plants, which changed and rejuvenated matter. Dix prayed that Xit wasn't going to attempt the anti-hydrogen method—a method he knew, with only his limited knowledge of physics, that converting matter into energy on the scale that perhaps Xit was considering would blow the *Auriga Lick* into total oblivion. A gulp brought a screen of blackness, blotting out any other thoughts.

Six

He must have fallen into the dark void of sleep. A soft, icy cold breath of air brushed his face; it was this sensation that had woke him. At first it didn't register that he had physically felt it. He had simply presumed he had thought it. Next he felt the palm of a warm hand gently pressing on his forehead. A woman's hand, soft and sensitive, as though the laying of it on his forehead could detect the beat of life.

The hand lifted, and Dix heard a sharp intake of breath and a cry from Irma. *Am I still thinking this?*" he wondered as his eye lids fluttered open. He didn't seem to have any control over their action. He heard coughs, cries, snorts, and sniffs of brief chuckles.

Then there was short, hesitant bursts of hand clapping interrupted with the beats of laughter and whoops of delight. After infinitesimal time, his eyes began to focus, and the milky white, diffused shapes melted into known forms: a grinning Xit wiping a tear from his eye, Jollity with his long fingers crossed over his mouth and his whole body hiccupping with delighted cackling, and Irma's face a bright light, every part of it dazzling, sparkling, and flashing, holding a mesmeric smile as though she had just witnessed a miracle. After turning his head slightly, he found Babe, Miss Algol, larger than he'd ever imagined her; she was flushed and shiny with perspiration, her arms held out towards him, looking proud as though she had just given birth.

He tried to sit up or raise his head, but this small, usually intuitive action defeated him, and immediately eight hands reached out to grab and hold him.

"Thank you," he gasped as he was sympathetically levered up into a sitting position. It seemed that telepathically his needs could be instantly read. "Thank you," he said again. His voice was a whisper, barely audible. "Thank you." Louder and stronger this time. "How did you . . . ?" Then he started to cry; it was spontaneous and totally uncontrollable.

He had wanted to ask them how, when one of the most sophisticated computerized systems in the galaxy had pronounced him dead; how had they, with not one grain of medical knowledge between them, managed to give him his life back, bring him back into the world.

"There, there, let it all out," Babe Algol said soothingly, her large hands gently caressing and tenderly stroking his head. "There, there."

He felt Xit and Jollity raising the back of the trolley up, felt pillows being tucked behind his back, and felt his nose and eyes being wiped with a tissue smelling of luscious roses.

He breathed an enormous sigh and felt the guilelessness of sleep sweeping over him. As it did he felt a smile pulling up the corners of his mouth, and his eyelids closing out the light. He felt contented and safe.

"Don't let him fall asleep," someone rasped far away in the fading distance.

"Keep him awake, for shrite's sake," a murmured, angry voice said, floating away.

"It's all right, it's all right, let him sleep. He's exhausted." This voice was a soothing whisper that allowed him to slip quietly away, unleashing him from the nagging, irrational feeling of responsibility.

Dix woke, instantly terrified that he was still dead. The bright light that exploded painfully and thudded into his frontal lobes snapped his eyes closed. The acrid stench of Xit's arm pit attacked every membrane in his nose, the ache in his shoulder, and the taste of stale, fermenting yeast scratching the back of his throat happily and gloriously announced that he wasn't deceased.

"He's awake," Xit joyfully sang out as though heralding a birth. At the same time, in deference to the sick patient, he took his elbow off the pillows where he had been resting it.

Dix could hear the creaking, stretching, and yawning of other sleepers waking up. He slowly opened his eyes and asked, "How long have . . . ?"

"Bloody days and days," Xit answered, cutting him off as he helped to raise him up. "Bloody days. Thought we'd lost you again, thought you'd bloody pegged it."

"Hello again, Mr. D," Jollity said, sniffing a wide, open smile while consciously putting on a pair of spectacles.

Dix nodded, smiled, and shook his head. Then he raised a finger and wagged it at the glasses, trying to say that everything had been forgotten, it was all in the past. Jollity frowned and didn't seem to understand, but before Dix could begin an explanation, Babe Algol loomed over him.

"How are you feeling?" she asked, pressing a hand onto his brow. "Better, then?" she answered her own question. "No fever." She took her hand away.

"Honest, you worried us so," Irma said, moving in and leaning over to slide her arms around him, pulling him closer to her in a big hug so that his head was held firmly against her breasts. He felt her heart pounding and listened to it, and he was surprised that he didn't feel the sickening revulsion he normally felt when she was this close to him. He was surprised that he didn't feel any kind of emotion except a kind of floating detachment.

"Let him be," Babe Algol gently admonished. "You're going to squeeze the life back out of him."

Irma abruptly unwound herself and moved back, apologizing in her girlie voice. "Sorry, Dix." Then she quickly corrected herself for some reason. "Sorry, Mr. Dannering."

"Listen," Xit said before Dix could ask Irma why she was being so formal. "You feeling up to it? Say if you don't, and we'll give you more time, but we . . . now you're awake?"

"I'm feeling fine, fantastic," Dix said with a grin. "Not sure I could do an entrechat at the moment, but fine." He saw a flicker of doubt on Babe Algol's face. "Honest." Then he realized that it wasn't doubt about his health that had furrowed her brow but a doubt about something else. "What is it?" he commanded more harshly than he meant to. "What is it?" he asked again more sympathetically.

He looked round at them, studying each one individually. They lowered their eyes not wanting to look into his. He turned to Xit, who didn't look away. "What is it, Xit? What's wrong?"

"You've been gone for a sizable amount of time."

Dix nodded. "Thought I had." Then more out of politeness than curiosity he asked, "How long?"

"Calendar and . . . several divisions."

"And?" Dix knew that time didn't mean anything; it wasn't unusual when travelling between planets to be in an induced sleep mode for long periods of time, from departures to arrivals. But being gone for a sizeable amount of time in this context meant that he hadn't been compos mentis when in an active mode.

He watched Xit as he carefully considered his answer.

"Well, he took over, just took over." Xit studied his hands. "Nobody challenged him, and he just . . ."

Dix knew instantly who Xit was talking about. "Popablu?" he rasped.

"Yeah." Xit gritted his teeth and sucked in a deep, hissing breath. "But no one calls him that anymore."

"So what do they call him?" Dix asked sardonically.

Xit glanced furtively at the others and then back to Dix. "Dix," he said quickly, barely opening his mouth and making a whistle and hiss.

"Dix!" It hit him between his eyes and the pit of his stomach, and it jolted him upright. "Dix?" He could hardly believe he'd heard it. "Dix?" he repeated slowly.

Xit nodded.

"Why?" He was still unable to totally believe or understand it.

"Said it was for continuity, for old times' sake, and that he wanted your name to be remembered." Xit shuffled and shrugged his non-comprehension or belief in the given explanation.

"And Dannering?" Dix whispered, stunned and hardly wanting to know. "He's using Dannering?"

"No, just Dix—calls himself Dix Dulipper."

A strangled sob from Dix made everyone stare at him questioningly.

"Dulipper?" repeated Dix, as though it was totally beyond his comprehension.

"Yes, Dulipper." The group was aware and curious that this meant something much more astounding than only using Dix. They all waited, unconsciously holding their breaths, searching his face for an explanation.

"Dix Dulipper," Dix whispered to himself, and then he gave a grunting snort of a derisive laugh. "Not content with taking over my ship, my troupe, he's taken over my name. How could he have known it?" He looked up and saw the bewilderment and the puzzled looks on their faces. "Dulipper is my second name—Dix Dulipper Dannering. My father gave it to me in a kind of tribute to Dix Dulipper Borradox, but I never used it and didn't know anyone knew about it." He shot a questioning look at Babe. "Except my dad and possibly my mother, whoever she was." He held his eyes on Babe. Either she was an amazing actress who could suppress her reactions and emotions in an instant, or the name didn't mean anything to her.

"Dulipper Borradox—who was he?" she asked, because it was obvious that Dix was questioning her.

"My father never mentioned him to you?" Dix probed.

She screwed up her eyes and tilted her head to one side, attempting to remember. Then she shook her head and pursed her lips.

Dix explained. "He was one of the greatest theatrical impresarios of the Theatre Palaces, a legend in show business, a man whom Dad admired more than anyone."

Babe Algol again shook her head, keeping her lips pursed and her brow creased in concentration.

"And you have never heard of him?" Dix asked accusingly, staring at her and unable to believe that his father wouldn't have mentioned it to her of all people. A thought jolted into him. "Unless, that is . . . ?" He held onto the thought as he searched her eyes for an answer to the question that he had never dared to ask. Then he flicked his eyes at Irma for the briefest moment, hoping for confirmation or denial on her face, but it only held puzzled interest. He looked back at Babe Algol.

"No . . . never heard of him," she said matter-of-factly. "And why should I have? Your father never discussed things with me—we were never that intimate."

"But you were lovers?" Dix gasped sharply, anxiously.

"Aw, that." Babe smiled. "Never lovers. Perhaps I loved him, but he never loved me. Perhaps I never really loved him; I just fell in love with the magic. I was very young." Babe looked away from Dix to give an explanation to the others. "I was very naïve but passionate about the theatre. One day I plucked up the courage, went to the back of the theatre, and asked a man at the stage door if I could watch a rehearsal. I didn't know who he was at the time."

Babe, for the first time in many years, remembered the red paint peeling off the stage door, the ruddy-faced man with a strong, long nose leaning against it, pensively tapping his fingers on his unshaven chin, his eyes sharp and alive but not focused on reality; they were focused somewhere beyond. Then when she had asked him her question, they had looked down at her and sparkled into bright blue awareness.

"For such a very beautiful princess, how could I resist? Come, come immediately, and I will show you the illusion and magic of theatre."

She remembered him guiding her round the back of the stage, past all the machinery and electronics, the wires and ropes that could trip up the unwary. He carefully lead her through them, and she was blind. Nothing registered until she was sitting in a box with its gilt seats, golden cherubs, and plush red velvet.

She gazed down. She was alone in the semi-darkness, and the empty seats below her curved away. She felt special and enormously precious like a pearl in the shell of an oyster. Then, as though the sun was rising, the darkness lifted and the stage shone out bright and brilliant. There in the centre was the man at the stage door—not the old, unshaven man with the ruddy face, but an elegant, tall prince bowing and smiling at her in a hooded red cape lined in white satin.

"For the brightest, most beautiful star in the galaxy, who has honoured our theatre, we offer you the most special of our gifts, magic and illusion." He had twirled away, his cape billowing as though it had caught the sky; wind, thunder, and music filled the theatre. Then like a magnificent butterfly, he flew back into the centre of the stage, and a bright light seemed to shine from him. "I am the emperor of illusion." He flung his cape wide, lights sparkling from it as he danced, and he kicked his legs high. "My boots." They seemed to slip off his feet and into his hands, and he held them up to her. "They are birds of love." He spun round, his cloak billowing out, and when he faced front again he held in his hands two beautiful doves. He brought them up to his lips and blew a kiss at them, sending both flying away.

Babe sat amazed, her eyes growing wider as he danced, spun, and twirled, removing individual pieces of clothing. His sequined waistcoat transformed into a beautiful peacock, its greenish iridescent tail displayed vain and glorious. His sparkling white linen shirt became a proud and noble swan, and his silver belt twisted into a lustrous serpent that he coiled around his neck.

She had given a little screech of embarrassment as she realized the only piece of clothing left were his trousers. She could still sense the hot blush as he looked straight up at her, giving a suggestive and wide smile. Then he whipped off his trousers and at the same imperceptible moment swung his cape round himself, half opening it to allow a small white goat to skip out.

She was totally mesmerized and transfixed when he then gave a deep, low bow to her, the hood slipping over his head. She remembered how she had sat there for a brief moment in total silence before jumping up to applaud, ecstatic with adoration. It seemed as though immediately arms were locked round her and whispered kisses were being brushed against her cheek. She remembered swivelling round and seeing him now dressed in a shimmering turquoise evening suit, and she'd thought it was impossible for it to be him when he was still bowing to her.

It was pure magic, and that was when she knew she was totally in love and wanted to be part of it. She had returned the kisses, intense and passionate, and had taken the first initiative, slipping off his jacket and unbuttoning the pearl buttons on his shirt. In the silence of the red velvet darkness they had made love—dazzling, wonderful, spontaneous love, soft and whispering at first and then burning with fiery, ecstatic energy.

When they finally pulled themselves apart, they quickly and furtively dressed. He had taken her hands, kissed them, and then gently brushed a lock of hair from her forehead. "May illusion, magic, and love last you forever"

Irma smiled and sighed. "Beautiful." Babe turned back to Dix. "No, we were never lovers. I made love to him, just once, but he never allowed it again."

Dix shook his head. Years of certainty evaporated, and he smiled weakly up at Babe and gripped her hand. "Irma, she is your daughter?" he asked quietly.

"Adopted. Never could conceive, not for lack of trying, though." She gently laughed. "Poor little mite had been abandoned; happened a lot during the wars."

The belly of Dix growled guiltily. His face glistened like wet leather, and he wiped a hand slowly across his brow as a thought came to him. *All these years, you thought she was your sister. You rejected her, spurned her, just because you'd fucked her one drink-besotted night. You're a . . .*

Another voice screeched, *Getting side-tracked! Forget about Babe being your mother, Irma your sister, all that sentimentality guilt trip. It's unimportant. Get your name and ship back.*

Was it a coincidence or what? Dix bit his lower lip. *He takes over the Auriga Lick, takes over the troupe, takes my name.* he licked his lips and tasted blood. *Whether he murdered you or tried to isn't important at the moment. Think logically.* He became agitated, annoyed, confused with the intermingling voices. He pulled his hand sharply away from Babe's as a voice commanded him to take it step by step.

"Why couldn't you hear what Docker was saying?" he snapped loudly and angrily, to dismiss the voices from his mind. Then he heard the words reverberating and piercing the silence of the corridors and saw the surprised, startled faces peering down at him. "Sorry, didn't mean it to come out like that." He shrugged apologetically.

The faces looked at him sympathetically.

"It was Docker that hit you, wasn't it?" Xit waited for Dix to nod. "The bastard, the lying bastard, knew he had," he snarled. "Knew it was that piece of dung—said so, didn't I?" The others nodded. "Knew it couldn't have been an unsecured counter-weight."

"Then everyone thought you were dead, thought you'd pegged it," Irma said, "Excepting Xit—he knew you weren't and convinced us that you weren't."

"You'd be on your way wrapped and trussed in a silver foil shroud by now, except for Xit." Babe breathed heavily.

Dix heard a slight accusation in her voice.

"Listen, I can't express my thanks enough," he said as he smiled up at her. "I'm not saying it's your fault in any way that Popablu has taken over. I just wanted to understand why my conversation with Docker wasn't heard or recorded." He looked at each one individually, trying to express his gratitude with a look rather than just words.

"Well," said Jollity, shuffling closer to Dix, "it's a long while ago, but I remember hearing the first bit coming through the tannoy." He stopped speaking, looked up at the ceiling, closed his eyes tight, and then said, "I remember it being something about Irma not being black, and then it all became kind of . . ." He searched for a word. "Muffled." He dropped his head down to look at his fingers, which had started rolling up the edge of the sheet on Dix's bed.

"Yeah, as if someone had put a hand over the mike," Irma said, and she demonstrated it with a screwed-up tissue, which she put into her mouth and started speaking.

"Shrites," Dix cursed, cutting Irma off. "Pissing shrites." He knew instantly in that moment what had happened. "Docker had moved closer to me, so I stepped back nearer to the mic, thinking he would be heard much more distinctly. But I must have got to close; I remember feeling it against my shoulder. Shrite." He saw that they wanted more explanation. "He was attempting blackmail." He quickly decided not to be to explicit about it, to save time. "He made a proposition that wasn't legit. He was a nasty piece of work, one of the most corrupt managers on Martios if not in the whole galaxy. I thought if I could expose him by everyone hearing what he was saying and also had it recorded, then he would lose his licence and everything . . ." The smell of almonds interrupted him fleetingly. "Now I remember it," Dix said to himself. "Just after Docker hit me. Who was the first to get to me?"

"Docker," Jollity said. "He was standing over you—seemed that he was first."

"Not Docker. After Docker."

They all hesitated and looked at each other.

"Not sure," Jollity finally replied. "We all seemed to arrive at once. Someone was there wrapping your head, trying to stop the blood."

"Popablu?" Dix asked, hoping for confirmation.

Jollity shook his head and shrugged that he didn't know. Then he said, "I remember that Xit was about last, because he pulled me out of the way to get to you."

"Was it Popablu bandaging my head?" He hoped that someone might confirm his suspicion and that the memory of almonds would make sense.

Jollity closed his eyes, attempting to visualize the scene again, but eventually he opened his eyes and shook his head.

Irma spat the ball of tissue paper from her mouth and caught it before it landed on the bed. "There was so much happening, I arrived just after old Kline, one of the fly men, and blood was everywhere." She made a swimming stroke with her hands. "People were slipping and sliding, falling over and wrestling each other to try and get a look at you; it was like a snake pit. You should have been there." Irma nodded emphatically and then realized what she had said. "Not dead, you understand—there, not dead. You know what I mean. Awake, alive." She got flustered, embarrassed, and angry with herself.

"Why does it matter? Why is it important?" Xit asked.

Dix heard the suspicious query in his question and decided, at the moment, not to explain his reasons for thinking that Popablu had attempted and nearly succeeded in murdering him. "It doesn't. I just had the feeling that it was him who got to me first." Then he quickly changed tactics to avoid any more discussion about it. "Was I immediately taken to the medical on *Auriga*?"

"Yes, I insisted," said Xit.

"They took him offstage to that medical room first," said Jollity slowly and deferentially to Xit. Then he hesitated before speaking again, holding his finger up as though he was trying to recall something more specific.

"That's right, that's right," gushed Irma excitedly. "I remember Kline helping me up, blood all over my hands, and then I got it all over my arse. We were following a line of people down those rickety steps; how they got you below stage without dropping you was amazing. They passed you over their heads from hand to hand, and you seemed to be floating."

Xit wiped his hand across his nose and sniffed. "Crap house, filthy, wasn't going to let them treat you there. Needed the best, needed to get you onto the *Auriga* as quickly as possible. He looked sternly at Jollity. "That hole didn't have any medical facilities." He said it as though repeating the defence of an old argument. Jollity blinked, nodded, and then turned to look straight at Dix.

"So you had me taken to the sick bay?" Dix said to Xit.

"No, no," Irma squealed enthusiastically, flapping her hands before Xit could answer, wanting to prove that she remembered the events in detail. "They had to float him back up the steps and onto the stage, I remember the bandaging round his head had come undone, and his blood was streaking everyone's face as they passed him along. They had to cross the stage, and those bastard miners started a slow hand clap as though it was some damned act."

"That was because one of those idiot sparks put a spot on him, before Mister Christel could get him into the airlock and aboard the *Auriga*," Babe said.

"It was beautiful, though," Irma sighed, "like a scene from a major production that you used to see at the grand theatres. Noble and majestic like a . . ." She stopped abruptly and waved her hands in front of her face apologetically. "Sorry, sorry, I . . ."

Dix shook his head and smiled kindly at her. He had decided not to ask any more questions. He was convinced that murder had been attempted, perhaps not on stage but more likely while he was unconscious in the sick bay on the *Auriga Lick*, where it would have been easy to keep him sedated and fix the computers to give out the negative readings. *How to prove it?* he asked, and then he answered himself. *Only one way, and that's to get back and examine the computers and then confront him.*

"I feel fit enough to return," he announced, starting to ease himself off the trolley. "From what you have told me, there is no doubt about it, if I am to regain command." He beamed a smile. "So if you would get my clothes." He swung thin, bony legs out of the sheets and over the edge of the trolley, expecting any moment a cheer and round of applause for his heroic action and determination to overcome his pain and bravely assert his rights.

There were no cheers or applause. He turned, half off the chromed sides of the trolley to look at them, and immediately his smile froze on his face as he caught their fleeting, shocked looks and awkward, shuffling embarrassment. "A problem? Something wrong with that?" He looked directly at Xit.

Xit gripped his bottom lip with a thumb and finger and started tugging at it, speaking at the same time. "Well, it's, err, not as bloody damned simple as that, not now."

Dix didn't say anything but gave a questioning raise of an eyebrow.

"When we got you out, we naturally thought that everyone was with us, thought the whole troupe and crew would back us." He paused briefly. "We knew we were breaking the law by doing it, but I knew you weren't dead. Irma, Jollity, and Miss Algol agreed with me."

"And you've been proved right," Dix said, tapping his chest and grinning.

"Yes, but in proving it we've been ostracized and alienated by the others." Xit stopped pulling his lip and said hurriedly, "They don't want you back." After a quick glance at the others he added, "The bastards."

Dix had stopped grinning and felt the muscles on his face becoming tight.

"We've all been threatened by them with a restricting order if we bring you back," said Babe Algol.

"Alive," Jollity added. "Dead's fine—they'd be happy with that, and we wouldn't be restricted."

"All of us have been included," sniffed Irma. "Babe as well. No one thought they could get rid of Babe." She snapped her fingers together. "Just like that." She fell silent and was close to tears.

Dix sighed, vaguely coming to terms with the fact that he wouldn't be returning like a conquering hero to take back the command of his ship and crew from the usurper and imposter. What he had a problem coming to terms with was the hard fact bursting and squirming into his mind: the rejection, the fact that he wasn't and hadn't been universally loved by everyone.

He had never consciously thought about it before and had taken it for granted. He felt hurt and belittled by it. The only ones who loved him and respected him were the four standing round his bed. He resisted the urge to grab hold of them and hug them, and he felt better. It was good to have loyal friends.

"Does anyone besides you four know that I'm alive?" he asked.

Xit, Jollity, and Irma looked quickly at Babe.

"No," She said, "I didn't speak to anyone. In fact the ones who saw me avoided me as though I was shrite."

"We all took turns in going back to replenish the provisions. Babe was the first to go after you had recovered," Xit explained.

"How have you been allowed to . . . ?" Dix didn't finish the question.

81

"Listen," Xit hissed apologetically, "I should have thought of just ejecting the silver foil shroud without you in it, but I didn't. I only thought of getting you out, getting you away from that bloody machine and its bloody diagnoses. I knew you weren't dead." He spun round to the others. "We had three sections to do it, three sections before he was going to be wrapped up."

"None of us are regretting it, Xit," Irma said soothingly. "Are we?"

"Definitely not," snapped Babe.

"No, you know that," said Jolitty with a nod and a grin.

Dix eased himself back onto the trolley. Another thought had him feeling irritated and incensed. He asked Xit, "Why did you of all people defer to him? Why did you allow him to take over? you were my natural successor—you should have been in command then, and none of this subterfuge would have happened."

Xit glared at him and breathed in deeply, clenching his fists.

"It was too late," Babe said, raising her hand and wagging a finger straight at Dix. "Popablu had taken over; he had established his authority during the time that Xit was looking after you." Then she folded her arms and took a deep breath. "He had tried, but it was you he was more concerned about than giving orders." She blasted out the last word and then followed it with an explosive crackle. "By the time he'd settled you in, seen that you were getting the best attention, Popablu had taken over as though he had been given the authority by the Corps." Then after breathing in deeply again to get her breath back she added quietly, "And you . . ."

Dix had stopped listening to her and didn't hear the last part; he had put his hand on Xit's. "I didn't mean to imply that you hadn't tried. I just find it bloody amazing that he seemed to be able to take over so easily."

Xit pulled his hand away. "I don't think he did it easily," he said. "I don't think he just took over. I think he's been working at it ever since he first arrived. And you," Xit added accusingly and angrily, "allowed it to happen."

Dix felt the thin needle of ancient, bitter, resentment pierce his heart. He swallowed hard, trying to relieve his throat, which had become dry and parched. "Me? How?" he managed to croak. "I detested the little bastard."

"You detested him? Don't make me laugh. Every time anyone complained about him, you sided with him, never reprimanded him, never castigated him. You never ever gave him a bollocking." Xit glared at him, his eye wide and bulging, purple and red veins marbled across it.

"He's right, you didn't," Babe challenged, sharply threatening as if about to strike him, her huge head jutting towards him and her smeared blue lips pulled back over her teeth. "Not one word of condemnation did you say to him, no matter how nasty or horrible he'd been. Especially to the two young chorus girls. Not one word. I gave up on you. I realize now that I shouldn't have, but I did; I thought it best just to ignore you, let you get on with it."

Irma squeaked scornfully, "Popablu, your blue-eyed boy. Every one of us stopped complaining about him to you; they knew it wouldn't get them anywhere. That's why we all knew and accepted that he was your choice, who you wanted to succeed you. Not Xit, who it should have been." She fought back tears but was still scornful. "I felt really relieved when I had heard that your life had ended, that I didn't have to pretend to be nice to you anymore just to keep my bloody spot. It was if a great weight had been lifted off my heart." She gulped back a massive sob before whispering, "Then he came." She nodded at Xit. "He persuaded me to help get you out for old times' sake, that there was a chance you might not be dead, that we had to save you at least till it was possible to get a second opinion." She burst into aggressive, gulping sobs. "I agreed—you bastard, I agreed."

Dix looked at them, their eyes glaring at him, and he started to speak but found he couldn't form the words because of the lump at the back of his throat. He swallowed to try to get rid of it, and he felt needles pricking his eyes, tasted the bitter sharpness of salt mixed with mucus seeping into his mouth. He felt his tongue darting out and licking his lips. If there was ever one time in his life that he had desperately wanted to die, it was now.

"I thought," he finally managed to rasp out slowly, the words tearing at his throat, "he was a spy, an informer for GEC. I didn't want to . . ." He stopped. He was going to say "upset him" and add that he wanted to keep him sweet for all their sakes, but he knew as soon as the words entered his head that they were just an excuse for his own selfish and despicable behaviour. It was a feeble excuse, and he knew it would seem like another lie.

What he desperately wanted to tell them was that he loved them and that now he realized how much he needed them. But he could find no words to express it that wouldn't diminish it, that didn't make it sound like a fawning, fatuous apology.

It was Jollity who broke the seething, scornful atmosphere, the maelstrom of venom that had boiled and erupted within the shimmering silver walls. "This is shrite," he said firmly, not looking at any of them. "Shrite's work." He was mumbling more to himself than the others. "Swelling, feeding off our brains. We are all in this together. We have faults, all of us, not just him." He did not look directly at Dix. "No good sulking, festering, scratching eyes out. Passion destroys intelligence. Let's forget it; it's been said, out in the open. Stop pissing on your possessions. Now we . . ." He took a long, slow, deep breath; put his hands up to his face; spread out his long, bony white fingers; and touched his ear lobes with his thumbs, his two little fingers pushing on the end of his nose. He closed his eyes and lifted his head up to the ceiling.

They all watched and waited for him to finish the sentence. In the silence that followed, they realized he wasn't going to finish the sentence and looked away, avoiding each other's eyes.

"He's right," Irma said finally, giving her nose a massive trumpeting blow, stretching out her long neck, and swallowing the saliva that had gathered in her mouth. "Not getting us anywhere. We have to be, err . . ." She sharply twisted her head round and up to Jollity.

"Pissing positive," he spat out to finish her sentence, not opening his eyes.

"Pissing positive." Irma blinked and stared at Xit, who was rubbing a finger round the socket of his false eye, a habit he'd acquired when he was trying to formulate his thoughts.

Xit stopped abruptly, sensing Irma's stare. "I haven't pissed positively for years." He glanced sternly back at her. She didn't notice his eye contained a glint of mischievous humour, and her mouth opened as she attempted to understand him.

A slow, hiccupping squeaking broke out from Jollitty, building into a crescendo of honking, cackling laughter. He threw his hands away from his face and out wide like a fluttering, demented bird.

It was infectious, and Babe caught it next after a brief glance down at Xit's sagging trousers that hid his catheter bag. Then she bounced and wobbled from a grin into a rasping, lip-vibrating laugh. Irma, bewildered and puzzled, started to laugh—simple, honest, naïve. She didn't know why but joined in because the others were doing it.

Dix dropped his head onto his chest to hide a smile, feeling that if he openly joined in, it might sour and spoil the intimacy of their shared moment. He had to bite his lip to stop his laughter from bursting out.

Then a beautiful, crystal clear sound reverberated through the labyrinth of Corridors. Xit laughed, genuinely laughed, which he rarely did. Most of the time the laughter that belched from his lips was sarcastic and derisive like the erupting bubbles of nebula methane. When he genuinely laughed, it was more of a high-pitched soprano giggle than an adult male chortle. You could hear the singing voice of the choirboy and the song he sang of the world held only in dreams and imagination. Xit's laughter conjured up beauty, magical moments, children dancing under sparkling lit waterfalls, and diving naked into deep pools of azure blue crystals. The sound filled the air with the trill and truthful moments of innocence.

This giggle, this peel of tinkling bells, stopped Dix's lip biting laughter and froze his whole body. A thought had hurtled into his mind, striking like a ball of lightning. It was a thought that held vengeful, burning, gleeful redemption.

Was it possible to achieve it? At that moment Dix didn't know, but he didn't even care—he was bewitched by the thought, imagining and visualizing it as it formed. The beginning, the middle, and the ending like a magnificently choreographed dance that held mystery in its performance, concealing the hard work that had made it possible, the bruised ankles and blood-soaked socks, the long, sweating hours in rehearsals working every step, breath, physical twist and turn to emphasize and counterpoint the music.

Dix imagined Popablu's assured and confident face breaking into shocked bewilderment, gasping in fear, his eyes clouding over dull and tarnished with no lights flashing in them, sobbing and pleading forgiveness upon seeing Dix's dream that was now a reality, that was tangible, solid, substantial.

He savoured every moment of this dream until it gradually distorted and transformed into the white rumpled sheets of the bed linen. Cackling with laughter, he carefully and diligently smoothed and straightened the folds and creases, and then he became aware that he could hear himself laughing, that all other laughter had stopped and breaths were being held. He sensed he was being stared at, and he lifted his head up and found them cautiously studying him as though he was demented and that at any moment he might become violent.

"You . . . screeched," said Babe hesitantly with a hint of fear. "Made us . . ." She gave a little shrugging jump.

Dix smiled and whispered softly, "I had a dream, a vision, an idea." He smiled. He could very clearly see Popablu, and he knew exactly where he would be. He knew exactly what the man was doing, and Dix knew exactly what he was going to do to regain the command of his ship, the respect of his troupe of Candle Dancers.

Seven

"I must be positive like Dix Dannering," Popablu said to himself, his silver blue eyes flashing in the spherical glass of the observatory.

It was exhilarating enjoyment being there, floating at the highest point on the *Auriga Lick* like a raindrop attached by a spider's thread to a pat of coprolite. He liked the solitary confinement, the isolation, watching the stars and planets slowly curving above and below him.

He growled sulkily, "Not that there's much to be positive about at the moment." Idly he looked at the liquid crystal display screens, reading out aloud and imitating the synthesized voice of the computer.

"Automatic pilot engaged. Majority of human personnel in sedated sleep patterns. Reproductions, androids, and sentinels in programmed mode for monitoring all human, electrical, magnetic, and mechanical requirements."

He turned down the contrast, and the lettering faintly glowed green, saying as he did. "Except for me and the four miscreants." Then he looked away and focused on his reflection in the oval glass, tilting his head to one side, his eyes sparkling like the distant stars.

"Dix Dulipper." he sang it out slowly, relishing using his real name, at the same time remembering it wasn't that long ago that it had made him feel restricted and never truly himself, and that if he ever did achieve anything, he would never have been sure that it hadn't been because of the family connections or that it was because he was the great-grandson of the legendary impresario Dix Dulipper Borradox.

"Stand or fall on my talent alone." The last words he angrily shouted at his mother and father before flouncing out, having made the momentous decision to go his own way and change his name.

He tilted his head backwards to gaze out into the universe, imagining that he was once more standing in front of his father. He mimicked his mocking, pompous, deep, gravel voice.

"And what have you achieved, my son, standing or falling on your talent alone? Are you a marquee name on the number one circuit, appearing in the Grande Palaces?"

"No, Papa," he answered with a boyish giggle, swivelling round in the chair, stopping abruptly, and booming out in his father's deep voice again.

"A rising star on the number two circuit?"

He swivelled back again to sing out in high soprano. "No, no, Papa dear."

Around again, dropping to the deep bass baritone, pushing out the words with the awful gusto of an amateur operatic diva.

"Then what are you? What have you achieved, my son, standing on your own two feet?"

Into a spin again, kicking off with great bellowing guffaw, then gleefully shouting out, "I am a singer with a troupe of Candle Dancers."

He imagined the look on his father's chemically sun-bronzed face, heard him screeching scornfully, gasping, cackling out. *"A singer? With a troupe of Candle Dancers?"*

He pushed himself round even faster, and the harmonious cosmos above him blurred into one silver streak, etched across the purple black blanket. He shouted out gleefully at the top of his voice, "Yes, yes, yes!" He allowed the chair to spin on its own till the revolutions gradually slowed down, and the universe broke back into the stars and planets. "Yes," he screeched out, flinging his arms out wide as the chair slowly ceased to spin.

A flashing, shimmering bright light flared across the dome, briefly illuminating the sphere and his naked body in a vicious red glow before fading away into the vacuum of space. A star had just burnt out, vanishing forever.

He felt enormously, yawningly sad knowing that part of his life was now over, that he was no longer a singer with a troupe of Candle Dancers, that now he was in command of an Auriga, the youngest person ever to achieve this status.

This would be seen by his sepia-coloured father, his waxen-faced mother, the congregation of aunts and uncles as success. He would be admired for working his way up, for his singular determination of doing it on his own, of standing on his own two feet. Of having done it without any patronage.

Promotion into the elite class and inner sanctum of GEC would be swift, a matter of course.

He smiled, drew his feet onto the seat of the chair folded his arms round his knees, kissed each of his white knee caps, and unconsciously hugged himself as he used to do as a child. He thought of the moment he had reverted back to using his family name; he knew that his adopted stage name was too flippant, lacking the authority for the position he had been given. It had been a relatively easy decision to make. Someone had inadvertently called him Dix during the Estoppel Xit episode, and without a second thought he had immediately and instinctively responded.

Others started to use it as if they were paying him a compliment, as if he had automatically assumed the mantle, the radiating aura of the governor.

It took him by surprise, how amazingly quickly they had accepted him, as though he had not only stepped into the shoes of Mr. Dix Dannering but had actually become the embodiment of him.

This at first amused and pleased him, and then he realised how fickle people were, how quickly they had changed their allegiance. It was as if the actual Mr. Dix Dannering had disappeared, had never existed.

He had felt very sad. He liked and admired Dix Dannering, who was more like a friend than the governor, who had taken him under his wing the moment he had joined the troupe of Candle Dancers. He hadn't known why Dix had done this; at first he had suspected that it was for an ulterior motive, that Dix Dannering enjoyed young pink flesh, but when nothing happened in this direction he gradually came to the conclusion that it was a genuine friendship.

Dix genuinely did like him and even considered him talented. He had never reprimanded him or condemned his actions, even after some of the troupe, mostly the females, had complained about him. They complained about his abnormal behaviour, and he didn't understand what this meant; it was never explained to him. He suspected that they were referring to some ancient codes of practice, old world cultural conduct that had long since disappeared.

When he had been on the casino's stage desperately trying to stem the blood spurting from Mr. Dannering's ears with both his hands, he had tried to thank him but quickly realized that it was useless; his words couldn't be heard. He tried to be gentle, tried with his thumbs to stroke Dannering's temple, hoping that this small action would be felt and that Mr. Dannering would know that he had been trying to help.

He had resisted taking command when it had been put to him by Mister Christel. "Xit's the natural successor, the most senior and the one nominated in the ship's articles," he had whispered, pointing at Estoppel Xit, who was totally obsessed with caring for Dix Dannering, becoming extremely angry—homicidal, even—if he was distracted for a moment from watching over the silent, still body.

"You have to accept the responsibility. No one else will," Mr. Christel finally said. "Decisions have to be made," He added curtly, as a matter of fact.

After several days of deliberating, he finally accepted. "Only on the understanding and condition that it is temporary, that I'm only the caretaker and will relinquish command as soon as Mr. Estoppel Xit wishes," he had stated, believing every word he had spoken.

"Or is certified rational," Mister Christel had added.

And that was how it remained until that dreaded, sleepless, nail-biting night, the night before he was going to have to take the awful action of waving his palm over the identification sensor pad that would activate the mechanism to jettison the great Dix Dannering into outer space.

The night when crashing and kicking Estoppel Xit had slammed into his room, practically psychotic, screeching that he had rescued Mr. Dannering, saved his life, stopped the callus murderers, the vindictive execution. Xit was going to bring him back to life.

"It's not possible." He had tried to reason with Estoppel Xit, feeling desperately sad. He felt like grabbing him, hugging him, wanting to stop the heartache, the grief, the pain he was suffering.

He didn't, knew he couldn't. He knew he was too young, too gauche, too inexperienced emotionally. He knew any attempt to comfort would be spurned and rejected with bitter, spitting hate. So he had just stood there letting the phlegm and spittle flick over him, not attempting to wipe it off or defend himself, as Estoppel Xit skipped backwards and forwards, yelling at him. He had held his breath to stop his tears, bit his lip till it bled to stop any sound of anger or sorrow escaping.

He had waited till Estoppel Xit had shrieked out of the room before allowing himself to cry. It didn't sink in what Estoppel Xit had done till Mr. Christel came to him and explained that the body of Dix Dannering had been taken from the sickbay. Then it sank in, and then he shouted and screamed at the insanity of such an appalling, useless action.

Later, while trying to emulate Dix Dannering, trying to live up to his reputation, his expertise, he had spent hours, days, weeks in the glossy panelled office. It had reminded him of his childhood, of another polished, fruity-smelling one where he had been taken by his parents to meet his relations, who had constantly patted him on his head. His cheeks were pinched by old men's callous hard, fishy, foreskin-feeling fingers. He had been perched on a massive desk, and a man sat behind it with a grinning, speckled blue face. Thin, knotted, knuckled hands had fondled his legs and then squeezed his knees so hard that he had cried out in pain, kicked out, then watched a streak of blood, the colour of walnuts, shoot out from the yellow teeth bared in the grey face.

He had been snatched up and shaken violently by his mother at the same time as his father had angrily slapped and hit him till his mouth and nose bled.

Later, after he had been let out of the cold, dark room into which he had been thrown, he had been told that he had kicked his great-grandfather, the legendary Dix Dulipper Borradox, in the mouth. He was probably the first and last being in the whole universe to do this. The old man had died soon after this incident. A blessing, his mother had whispered, telling him that the old goat never forgot or forgave even if they were kith and kin.

The desk in Dannering's office was identical to Dulippers. Popablu had sat at it, stroked and caressed it for many hours, hoping that it would give him confidence.

He had walked round and round the room, touching and feeling everything and desperately hoping that something would rub off, seep into him from the fabric and texture of the objects, give him the courage and confidence that he desperately required.

It didn't.

Then, mortified, he discovered that everything in the room was mock, imitation; even the solid wood desk was painted and veneered papier-mâché. The mosaic floor was a cleverly painted scenic cloth, highly varnished to make it shine like polished marble. It had appalled him that everything was imitation, a delusion. He felt cheated and felt that his hero, Mr. Dix Dannering, had cheated and deluded him.

He stopped going to the office and ordered that it be sealed. He preferred the observatory, with its real diamond, woven, black lacquered units, and the large animal hide seat, soft and smooth into which he could sink, feel it envelope and caress his naked body. Here in the bubble, he felt reborn; he had no need to imitate anyone and could be himself.

He watched a shooting star silently streaking alongside the sphere, remembering how hard he had wished and hoped that Estoppel Xit was right, that Dix Dannering was alive, that there had been a malfunction in the medical bay's computer, that Dix Dannering would wake up and retake command of the *Auriga Lick*.

But gradually and through the many checks and double-checks Mr. Christel had carried out, he knew there hadn't been a malfunction, that the machine's diagnosis was correct.

Estoppel Xit had stepped beyond all boundaries of the law, had blatantly and wilfully broken the cardinal rule of intergalactic space travel. There would be no redemption; he would never ever now take command.

The shooting star silently and instantly vanished. There was no spectacular pyrotechnical explosion.

"The apprehending of the four miscreants and the return of the body of Mr. Dix Dannering was not of immediate concern," he had informed all the members of the troupe when addressing them in regard to the incident. "I am prepared to wait; they have nowhere to go. My concern is that the body be returned so that it can be given a respectful and fitting farewell. It was the least he deserved." There had been applause, and he had nodded graciously in acceptance of it.

He had not added to his little emotional speech the fact that his concern was more to do with himself and the position he now held. He wanted a clean break from the past and a definite, clear beginning with no loose ends; the jettisoning of the body would have helped. It wasn't meant to be disrespectful, but if he could have given a suitable and fitting farewell, this would confirm that he was totally, unequivocally in command of the *Auriga Lick* and the Candle Dancers. He wanted there to be no doubt, no uncertainty when he informed his mater and pater.

He didn't want to apprehend the four miscreants, either; apprehension would imply that they were criminals. No, he wanted them back, wanted them to return of their own free will. He wanted them back in the production. Selfish? Yes. If they were not on the billing, in the running order, then the troupe would be debilitated and probably, almost certainly, not be allowed to perform at the next venue.

He knew their worth, their contribution. But how to get them to return was another matter, and he had had no ideas on how to achieve it. His secret hope, which he would never divulge to another soul, was that the body, removed from the balanced atmosphere of the medical pod, would quickly start to decompose. He prayed that would bring them back.

"Now," he said to himself, taking his legs from under his chin and crossing them under him. "I would of course change the line-up—I would have to, perhaps give them all larger billings. Keep Babe Algol number one obviously." He briefly squeezed his nose. "Put Jollity Strad at the head." He visualised Strad held in the white circle of the spotlight, sloping onto the stage, not speaking, not acknowledging the audience, nonchalantly peering round as though it was the first time he had been in such a place, and then suddenly becoming aware that he was being watched by the audience and leap back with a skip and a hop, bellowing with surprise.

"Yah . . . Sorry . . . Sorry." He'd stutter apologetically. "I was just looking for some, you know, for somewhere. I'd been told that there was a place where you could get two free tots of star juice, sex with the most gorgeous girls in the universe, and a pie." He waited a beat for this incredible bargain to be recognised before wheezing, "And I was just wondering what kind of pies they were."

He smiled to himself, listening once more to one of Strad's old jokes. Then he sighed and felt despondent because he knew what Strad would say if he even dared suggest his idea to him: that he, the great Jollity Strad was to take the opening spot. He cringed as he heard the tirade.

"What? You want me to step out onto a cold stage? Step out before the wicks on the candles were stable, before they had caught hold and were up to brightness, before the bloody punter's bums have had chance to warm their bloody seats? Before they had stopped shuffling their bags, tunics, before they could find the right way to crane their necks to see round the heads in front of them? Before Zerk had warmed up his spot, let alone finding out where he should point it? Not a bloody warm-up man, am I? You can stuff it. Sorry, but you can stuff it all the way up your tight little rectum."

And he would be right. *But how can I make it my show, give it my identity, let everyone know that Dix Dulipper has arrived?*

The *Auriga Lick* was now travelling close to the skin of the universe; there were no stars spinning by, just the soft velvet blackness of nothing.

"I'll sleep on it," he said with a sigh. He was tired of the numerous problems that surfaced and needed attention if he was going create his new personalised, dynamic show.

He swivelled in his chair and let the nothingness curl him to sleep.

Eight

$\mathcal{D}$ix Dannering was not aware they were travelling near the skin of the universe.

He was aware that it had been incredibly hard and frustrating to get Xit, Jollity, Babe, and Irmal to agree to his idea, to understand his dream. "It's what I want—now do it." His old adage was no longer accepted or tolerated.

They no longer accepted that his word was paramount; he was no longer the supreme authority, the governor. They had argued and introduced their own ideas and opinions, and it had taken days of discussion and negotiations to finally get them to accept that his way was right, that what he wanted to do was right. And even after an agreement had been reached, there had still been pockets of resistance that had to be discussed and negotiated.

But now it was finished, now his dream had been realised and was reality. He stood proudly in front of it and could only smile, pleased and amazed at what they had achieved. Xit kicked like a fly with a broken leg over to him. "Yeah what, bloody yeah, didn't believe it could be done, didn't believe it. No way, no bloody way, but bloody marvellous, supreme." He punched Dix on his shoulder. "You the bloody governor again."

"A day to get the lights rigged and the cameras warmed up, and then we'll transmit." Dix couldn't help the grin on his face. The cameras, monitors, and transmission equipment had been dismantled from the gun decks and then cleaned, checked, and aligned for exposure, system timing, and black levels. Amazingly they still worked.

"Governor this is what this bloody business is about. Used to be about before his fuckin' ilk took over."

Babe, with an arm round Irma's waist, swayed over to them. They both were smiling and shaking their heads in admiration. Babe huffed a short laugh. "Didn't think it was possible, not at all possible."

"But we did it, we did it." Dix beamed, stroking his bald shiny dome. "Just got to get the lighting right to make it come alive."

Babe took her arm away from Irma. "You're a chip off the old block; if he could do it, you can do it." She wagged a fat stubby finger at him.

"He couldn't have done what you've done," chirped Irma.

"Not no way."

Xit said, "Yeah, but now it needs to be lit, and he had Stun." He squeezed his fingers against his skull.

"Stun," Babe repeated, snorting a derisive laugh. "Your father could do it without Stun—didn't need him. Don't you remember when he went missing? He had us all doing it, even Xit."

"Even Xit?" Xit hissed, hurt and angry. "You fat fuck . . ."

Babe laughed, cutting him off. "Come on, Xit you weren't the most balletic trapeze artist."

"Bloody barn door up your back passage, and you wouldn't be either."

"It was hilarious." She turned to Irma. "There we all were, swarming all over the grid, and there was suddenly this almighty screeching, and then there he was." She nodded and grinned at Xit. "He flew across the stage, arms and legs flapping, knocking into all the lamps, and—"

"And his bloody father," Xit shrieked with laughter. "His bloody father yelling up at me. Fuckin' apoplectic, he was. 'Mind the fuckin' lights, you brainless idiot, mind the fuckin' lights!'" Xit shook his head and sniffed. "Mind the fuckin' lights. He didn't give a toss about me with a hot barn door jammed up my butt."

"He was like a demented spider running round the stage underneath us and screeching up at Xit." Babe raised herself up on her small, pointed feet and waved her corpulent arms, mimicking Dix's father.

"Yeah." Xit shook his head, smiling at the memory. "We did it though, didn't we?"

Babe stopped wobbling and nodded. "We did, and we'll do it again." She turned to face Dix. "Just tell us what you want, where you want them, and we'll dress them in for you, just like the old days."

Dix looked at them, and then he glanced over at Jollity Strad fast asleep on a mound of unused cut cloths taken with the rest of the scenery out of the bay. *These four,* he mused to himself. *A tired, exhausted comedian who became breathless on his first attempt to tie a hemp line onto a barrel. A thin, skeletal old man with one eye, a withered leg, and a catheter bag strapped to his groin. A fat, pink blob of lard who couldn't raise her arms above her head. And physically the most fit, the most agile of them all, perhaps of all the troupe, who could swing with grace and ease across the lighting grid with pure, perfect agility. But perhaps—no, not perhaps, but definitely . . ."* Irma smiled coyly back at him, her trusting, cow-like eyes opening wide. *Definitely the least intelligent of the whole troupe. she wouldn't have one iota what was required if she was not given direction.* He smiled back at her, then at Xit and Babe. *These four are going to be my sparks, the brushes that will paint the light to give my tableau life.* Although he still held his smile, he could feel the despair making a tangled knot in his stomach. His smile became a fixed grin, changing slowly and imperceptibly into a grotesque, grimacing gargoyle.

Xit's voice sang out. "And that should have the bastard, Mr. Almighty Popablu blue eyes, cut down to size. We'll show him what show business is about, show him an extravaganza that he will never have seen before, never dreamed of. Show him who's the master, the governor."

The others laughed and clapped their hands enthusiastically, caught and trapped in their own creation and an achievement that they had not thought possible. Jollity woke up, rubbed his eyes, and smiled.

The knot in Dix's stomach immediately unravelled, and the gargoyle grimace vanished. Lips parted, teeth opened, head threw back, eyes sparkled, and hands smacked together. His laughter filled and echoed through the bowels of the *Auriga Lick.* He had been given back the reason to succeed.

Nine

"You will succeed," his voice screeched, high pitched and strident. Every purple blood vessel on his iridium-coloured face pulsated, and his thin, wiry body was stretched and taut. The words held venom, anger, and total frustration that could desecrate loved ones, destroy families, tear down society.

It was a command from the most powerful man in the universe.

Power that was now frustrated. Power that might be losing its grip. Bellowing, snorting power, stamping feet, fist-beating desk power. Wounded power that killed the obedient, killed the sycophants, blindly killed friends, family, and anything weak or strong that held any threat. Power that had to hold onto its dominance, otherwise it would lose.

"You will succeed." The voice was softer, piercing, creaking ice.

"And if, as I said before." A reply delivered quietly, simply, matter-of-factly. "If I don't succeed, if it is impossible to succeed?"

The room, full of every member of the GEC Inner Council, stopped breathing; their eyes and thoughts were focused on the solitary figure standing in front of them and facing one of the most powerful figures in their worlds. If they could have summoned all the kinetic forces in the universe to remove this, lone, solitary person who dared challenge his, their authority, they would have done it.

The nominated figure head of the most powerful beings in the galaxy sighed, shrugged, and sat down. "Then we have lost," he said softly. "Entire fleets will be lost. The population of our worlds will be decimated through this most flagitious act." He gave a deliberate pause; there was no emotion, no controlled eruption of blood vessels. "The truth." A pause. "It comes down to this." He snorted a breath. "I don't like being fucking duped. I want to know why I was fucking duped. By who, for what?" His eyes, face, and hair were cinder grey, and his hands were like a steel hawser twisted into an anchor.

"And if I don't succeed?" The repeated question was more whispered than stated.

"You, Detective Inspector Chapter Editor," was hissed in reply. There was controlled, seething hatred of the person in front of him. "I am told you are the best." His cinder grey eyes flicked upwards, and his whole body expressed the hate and loathing he felt for this person in front of him, having to admit that he needed her—this irritating little dung beetle, a mere woman who dared to challenge him.

"My question remains unanswered."

The eyes flicked down. "Shit, you try my patience." Perhaps a glimmer of respect. "I give you my word." A glint of total, unequivocal malevolence. "If you fail, there will be no"—he gave an emphasised pause, looking round with his lizard head to the assembled GEC members "—no retribution, no retaliation, no punitive revenge."

"I want better than your word. I want definite." There was stunned silence as Detective Inspector Chapter Editor continued. "Words."

She looked directly into the cinder grey eyes. "I love you, I hate you," was barely audible to the audience behind her, who were squirming in their seats that a woman dare challenge his words.

She was the first woman ever in the police force to reach that rank. On receiving the promotion, she was given the nickname Dice by her intimate colleagues and friends, who all felt that in some way they had helped her achieve it. They had, within the first month—when they no longer felt on friendly intimate terms, no longer comrades, no longer kindred spirits—dropped the "D" off her nickname. She became known as Ice.

She accepted it as a compliment. It was during this period that her fine, silky long hair had turned bleach white. She immediately had it shaved off, leaving her with a head of delicate gossamer. Because of the other features on her face—the thin, sharp, hooked nose; the high cheekbones; the small eyes the colour of burnished bronze set in deep, round sockets—she had the look of a gosling. Wigs were established quickly before a new nickname, "Duck Head", could be applied. Ice stayed.

"Words, do they mean anything? No, not unless it is supported by something tangible, some action that defines love, defines hate. Give me something tangible, something more than just your word."

The eyelids fluttered across the burning cinders, a dark brown tongue curled out and flicked across yellow teeth.

"Tangible, tangible." The lids of his eyes held closed, and his head waved from side to side. "This is tangible. Nothing else. We have tangible, we own it, we hold it, we make it work." His eyes shot open, and his reptilian head thrust forward. "There is nothing tangible for you. You don't have the power, I—" He stopped abruptly, swivelling his head and scrawny vulture's neck to the gathered members, slowly stretching his arms out and twisting the palms of his hands upwards, not totally in flat supplication; an incomplete gesture. "We, we hold order. We have total, unequivocal power in the palms of our hands."

The applause from the assembled GEC members was a thunderclap, immediate and with no hesitation.

Detective Inspector Chapter Editor, standing in front of this man, wished at that moment that she could have stopped breaking wind, stopped the expulsion of the gaseous air that billowed through her underwear, stopped the rapid squall, the sudden and violent gusts of farts that had been contained and held successfully till this moment, when they announced themselves, bellowing and trumpeting, through her fine wool, white trousers. The applause died away as the crescendo of gaseous farts progressed to a climax.

His head pulled back into the shoulders, and his hands came together into the steel hawser anchor; grey, burning cinder eyes flicked at the detective. "Something you ate?" he said, "or a flatulent expression of your opinion regarding this assembly?"

"Neither." She hoped her bowels had finished the concerto. "Probably something I drank."

"The fountain in the orangey, while you were waiting?"

Detective Chapter Editor nodded and swallowed.

The old man pulled his head out of his shoulders, and a thin smile pulled at his mouth. "It is untreated. Noxious emanation, miasma. It looks beautiful—sparkling delicious, cascading purity." He paused to lick his lips. "Poison. A few incandescent drops can make your bowels into a boiling cauldron of erupting sulphuric gas." The slither of a smile turned into a glinting stiletto, and his voice became harsh and sharp. "All present in this room know what I am about to tell you. There will be no suppressio veri. You understand?"

"Suppressio veri?" Chapter asked, anus cheeks clamped together, hoping to stop any more involuntary eruptions.

"Suppression of the truth, misrepresentation by concealment of facts that ought to be made known." He sucked in through clenched teeth. "Sometimes, on occasions we have had to do it for the good of the world, the universe—suppress the truth." His grey eyes locked onto hers. "But mostly we do it to hold onto power. The power that gives us our wealth and comfort, that enables us to have the good things in life." The thin, sardonic smile returned. "You now have the truth."

With those words Ice began to melt. Chapter Editor knew she had no bargaining power; she was condemned. They held the power of life and death, these chosen few. She wished she had now chosen the blonde wig instead of the pearl black one, which she knew would now emphasise her bone-white face even more now that all the blood had drained out of it. He would know he had frightened her.

What the hell—you are Detective Inspector Chapter Editor, she said to herself. *Retirement was heart-achingly boring.* This thought brought the hint of colour back into her face. *I was bored to death. The years of pottering mindlessly about are about to end, at least for the immediate future. It now seems my skills are once again required. They need a detective. It must mean that their deviant network of spies, their brutal barbaric police and Sturm troopers, have failed.* She smoothed down the lapels of her black jacket and checked the top button of her cream silk blouse.

The man staring down at her must have, by some imperceptible movement, given a command; the wall behind him began to slide down revealing a large, liquid crystal screen. At a slight twitch of his finger, the screen came alive with the most dazzling, beautiful image that Chapter Editor had ever seen in her whole life. In the foreground golden sunlight picked out intricate lattice arches laced with climbing roses of every hue and colour; a lapis lazuli sea sparkled and lapped against the edges of a landscaped garden. Topiary hedges lined white-gravelled paths, and trees of every variety, some dripping with fruit and others feathered in blossom, reached up into the light blue sky. Terraced areas held wild gardens with shrubs and silver-barked saplings with drifts of moon daisies and bluebells. Vibrant azaleas spilt onto a sparkling stream flowing into an eye-dazzling silver lake, flashing in the distance. It was magical. Chapter caught her breath, a long forgotten memory woke in her mind. A small girl with long, blonde, fine, silky hair peering at an old biscuit tin lid with a rusty dent in the middle; printed on it had been a scene similar to the one she was seeing now. "Where is this pretty place, Mummy?" the girl was asking.

"From someone's imagination, I expect."

"It's very pretty. How can you imagine something so pretty?"

"It is said that a long time ago, even before your great, great grandfather was born, our world and the planet looked a bit liked that. Maybe it did, maybe it didn't. Now, throw the dirty thing away—you have a lesson to go to."

A voice scratched away her memories. "We need you to find the perpetrators of this." She focused on the cinder grey eyes and the fiery orange pupils. "This," he snarled, "could bring us to the bottom of the honey pot. All of us here will survive, and survive well, but there will be no inheritance. We will be the last survivors, and after us there will be nothing left. As for the rest . . ." He gave the meanest shrug of his shoulders. "The citizens, the workers of our planets on whom we depend to gather the nectar and keep the pot full, to whom we give life and a reason to live—they will not survive for long after our patronage has ceased. Unless." His eyes closed briefly, and he raised his hand and flapped it as though fanning away some foul odour. His eyes opened again. "That, Detective Inspector Chapter Editor is your assignment, and the reason you were brought out of retirement. You will be given all the appropriate resources and anything else that you require to be successful in this mission." The hand stopped flapping, and the wall behind him closed over the magical, beautiful landscape.

The meeting was finished, and his eyes closed. His body sat rigidly still and began to fade away; the rest of the members of the GEC also faded away.

She was left alone in a dark, cavernous room.

"So this is how you conduct your intimate briefings, as fucking holograms," she shouted before sighing. "Clever, though—no chance of any physical attacks. But I should have suspected something. Must be retirement rusty." She turned and then turned around again, looking for a way out. A small, hardly distinct red light pulstated and seemed to indicate an exit. She moved towards it.

Below the red dot a door silently opened, and bright light exploded into the room, making Chapter blink. The silhouette of a man appeared.

"Miss Editor, ma'am, you follow me, please." The man waited till Chapter had crossed to him.

"Where to?" Chapter asked.

"Sorry, I have not the facility to answer questions. You follow me, please."

Chapter shrugged. "Okay, whatever." She knew that the man was a programmed android. It moved off, and Chapter obediently followed.

After the darkness of the cavernous chamber, the bright, buttery light gave her spirits a lift. She had been feeling a bit down, a bit depressed, but now her old self started to return, and she felt energetic physically and mentally. She noticed, as they moved through the glass walls of the corridor, that gardens, waterfalls, and cultivated fields continued to the horizon, and animals grazed. Except for not having the lapis lazuli sea, it had a remarkable resemblance to the recent images she had just witnessed. Above her soared a massive geodesic dome, and rain clouds drifted across webbing.

Just as pretty, she thought, and then she cynically corrected the thought. *Perhaps just another hologram.*

The android stopped at a set of tall double doors made, in contrast to the glass and steel corridor, out of dark, roughly hewn wood from a bygone era; the ornate hinges depicting mythical creatures were made of black, pitted iron, and the emblem of the Corps was embedded in them. The huge doors swung open, and as they did the android stepped aside and gestured for Chapter to enter. When she did, the doors closed silently behind her; a sonorous clunk signalled they were closed and locked.

The room was simply furnished, the floor was of tumbled marble, the walls were painted in off white, and the light was gentle and soft and seemed to have no direct source. A circle of armchairs was positioned in the centre of the room, and two men rose to greet her. "Miss Editor, would you mind if we had a few moments more of your time?" one of them asked, his voice smooth and cultivated.

"Did you appreciate the show?" the other one said. He had a similar voice, and he gestured to an armchair opposite theirs. "Please."

She nodded, smiled, and moved towards the proffered seat, subconsciously noting that her rubberised soled shoes made no sound as she walked. *Sound dead, no resonance,* she said to herself, wondering why.

The two men moved to her, their hands outstretched, their faces not chemically bronzed but naturally tanned with a sheen of oil, holding distant and patrician expressions. "To prove we are not holograms." They shook hands with her, beaming white-teethed smiles before making another seating gesture. They waited politely for her to sit and then sat themselves.

They both wore white linen kaftans over formal, dark grey silk suits. Both had highly polished black shoes with no socks, and their faces were framed with black shiny hair. Their lugubrious body language was relaxed, calm, and assured. Both began speaking at once and then apologised to each other, then to Chapter.

"Sorry."

"Yes, sorry." It was delivered with an apologetic laugh from the one on her left.

"It was a test," said the one on her right. "The hologram exercise."

Left said, "We thought you might have suspected?"

Right asked, "And you didn't?"

Chapter shook her head "No," to the Right. "No," to the left, with a slight shrug. Then before either of them could speak again, she said, "Would you mind me asking who you are? I feel at a slight disadvantage."

They both laughed. "Sorry, sorry, quite forgot the formalities. This is my brother, Arcanum Bix Bieder, and I'm—"

"Trunnion Bix Bieder." Chapter interrupted, embarrassed by not recognising them instantly. "Sir," she gulped, "I apologise. I'm very sorry that I didn't immediately recognise either of you. Please accept my apologies."

How could I have been so stupid? she thought. *Images of them are framed in every government office throughout the universe. Any important announcements on televised news bulletin was reported in front of their pictures. How do you address these people, who have the power of life and death over you? Do I stay sitting, or should I stand? I shouldn't have worn these stupid white trousers.* Her thoughts tumbled.

"Please, Miss Editor, it is we who should apologise," Arcanum said.

"Yes, we should not have played that game with you. We should have been straightforward, in the open. Do accept our sincere apologies." A smile, with head slightly cocked to one side. A hand gestured in friendship, waiting for Chapter to accept their apologies.

Chapter smiled. "Thank you. I feel a little out of my depth." She felt she was drowning, her chest felt tight, and she opened her mouth wider to draw in more air.

"Our reputation precedes us, but not everything that you have probably heard about us is true."

"We are quite benign."

Benign like hibernating scorpions, Chapter thought to herself, recovering her composure. *The silk blouse was a good addition—helps emphasise the boobs, perhaps give me an edge.* But this thought was immediately suppressed because she had seen no sparkle of sensual appreciation or attraction in the men's eyes. She smiled sweetly and nodded.

"Good, then let us enlighten you in regard to requesting this face-to-face meeting."

"We believe the hologram theatrical was a misconceived idea. We thought the essence of it would give a strong visual impact to this incident and emphasise our concern."

"We simply want to know who created the scenes you observed, and for what reason they were created."

"At first we thought someone from this, our own environment, had made it. There were similarities, but after extensive viewings and analysis, the conclusion arrived at was that the visual images had been taken from somewhere else."

"And that the story of the two space navigators receiving the transmission by accident, as they travelled along the skin of the universe, was true."

"Although our scientific boffins are in debate about the recording . . ."

"The images were seemingly transmitted on one system and recorded by another. We are told that this would be electronically impossible, because of the linear programming." He referred to a file on the arm of his chair.

"But we are also informed that an interference—say, an electrical storm—could possibly have made it occur."

"We have all the data for you."

Chapter waited for a moment before speaking, assessing the situation and the two very charming men. She decided to be direct. "I will start by interviewing the two space navigators, if—"

She was stopped speaking by a raised hand.

"I'm afraid that will not be possible."

Chapter lifted her eye brows questioningly.

"The local authorities at their port of arrival interviewed them, and I am afraid they were rather overzealous in the pursuit of the information we required."

"They killed them," Chapter said derisively.

"Unfortunately they died during the interview, yes."

"You have their interviews?" She tried to keep the contempt she felt for the new Sturm guards and their methods out of her voice.

"It will be possible for you to have the recordings. There wasn't very much to gleam from them; they were very vague."

Not surprising, thought Chapter, *when thugs were beating you to a pulp.*

"But the harm they did could be catastrophic."

"Quite," Chapter said curtly.

"I don't mean the authorities." The charm in Trunnion's voice had disappeared. "The space navigators. The recordings should have been automatically given to a superior who would have assessed its worth and, if he felt it warranted it, passed it upwards for more detailed analysis. Instead, the idiotic navigators decided, for reason known only to themselves, to break the law."

Arcanum explained. "All information that space navigators collect, every piece of data and every recording, is the property of the state." His voice was measured and controlled. "We have experts who can evaluate this information, assesses the importance of it and whether any or what action need be taken."

"These two thieving scoundrels purloined it and probably sold it to a casino manager, a so-called friend of theirs, who promptly transmitted it on his casino's internal viewing screens."

"What happened next was like wild fire."

"We still don't clearly understand how it was possible."

"How was it possible for such a mass exodus to happen? The question baffles us and leaves us bewildered."

"You have a network of spies. Did they not inform you of the circumstances?" Chapter asked innocently, but she was as bewildered as they had said they were. The vast network of spies they employed, and the coercion applied on every citizen in the universe to inform on each other hadn't, in this case hadn't worked. It seemed unbelievable.

"We believe the dream was too great."

"The dream being . . . ?" asked Chapter tentatively. Then she answered her own question with a laugh of incredulity. "That there is a place, a world, like the one depicted?"

Arcanum and Trunnion nodded together.

Trunnion continued. "It is nonsense of course. If there had been such a world, it would have been discovered by our astrologers long before now."

"We believe it to be totally fabricated, fake, created and conjured up by some malcontents who feel they have a grievance against us, who wish to create havoc—and who have so far, unbelievably, achieved just that."

A woman whom Chapter hadn't been aware of appeared from somewhere behind her and crossed silently to the brothers with a file of papers that required signing. She whispered in turn to each of the brothers.

Chapter laughed to herself and mused cynically as she carefully watched the two men. *Who is it that they feel has a grievance against them? Now, who would that be?* She was careful not to stare at the two men. *Perhaps your colleagues, whom you dominate through a mixture of blackmail and terror. The millions of relatives of the people you put to death in horrible ways. The people against whom you used your distinctive form of terror, being coerced into the exercise of criticism and self-criticism by which they were forced to confess and implicate each other in terrible wrongs. The people confined to their work units in the cities and villages, too terrified to speak out.* She felt an angry blush creeping over her face. *No, it is not difficult to believe that there would be any malcontents attempting to subvert your rule or disagree with you. You and your cohorts, living in a green and pleasant land, while they are scratching a living in the mines*

107

and are poisoned by the atmospheric conditions in the factories, their homes. Any bloody tyrant can solve the problems of political uprising if they are prepared to sacrifice all considerations of humanity and trample down all constitutional and judicial rights, and . . . Her thoughts were interrupted when the woman moved away with the signed file of papers.

"She has the ability of thought transference, Miss Editor," Arcanum said languidly, finishing reading a sheet of paper the woman had left with him and looking up, his face and eyes expressionless.

Once again Chapter wished she hadn't been wearing the black wig, realising at the same time why there had been no noise from her footsteps: the non-resonance would help in the transference of her thoughts.

"She read my thoughts?" She laughed, thinking quickly and making it sound amused, not serious.

"Yes. You think it's amusing?" Arcanum's eyes held hers.

Attack was the best form of defence. "Whatever thoughts of mine she transferred would have had no valuation or conclusion." She nodded at the sheet of paper.

"Which are . . . ?" Trunnion asked, tapping his fingers on the arm of his chair.

"You have enemies," Chapter answered quickly. "Why do you have enemies? It's rhetorical. Because of the methods used to suppress any aggression or threat to your personal power."

"Any misdemeanour is normally dealt with," Trunnion stated. "This one, at first, seemed to lack any malice or cause us any concern." He paused briefly. "Except for the breach of trust. It seemed to carry no personal threat. It would have been difficult to comprehend that it would cause so much disorder, havoc, and threat—not only personal, but to this actual existence and life order." He paused again. "This pebble thrown in a pond didn't create ripples but a tsunami."

Arcanum took over, although it was difficult to distinguish one from the other because their speech patterns were identical. Both spoke moderately quickly, paused frequently, and were not animated. "We did not create this world, this universe we now inhabit, and neither did our fathers or our fathers' fathers." His eyes held Chapter's for a moment. "They and we have learnt to adapt to it. We've invented ways and means of surviving."

"The world and the planets became infirm long before we took over. They were poisoned and polluted by people who were careless of the catastrophe they were creating." He flicked his tongue across his lips. "Even though they were given warnings through the climate changes, the depleted ozone layers, and the evaporation of the seas, they were greedy and heedless of the future. We, the beneficiary of their wantonness, have learnt to live and adapt to their legacies."

"Although our environment is artificial, it is what we have conceived, created, and built. Anyone could have done it, but it was our ancestors who had the foresight to pursue and build it."

"The navigators sold their navigational logs," Trunnion said, bringing it back to the reason why Chapter was there. "We know they were copied and sold again. Most of them have been traced, including the originals; the ones who bought them have been interviewed. But a few of the copies have disappeared."

"An exodus started. Ships were taken—some stolen or commandeered, some totally voluntary. The population of this galaxy is being depleted; factories and mines are closing down because of this. The source of our revenue is being starved, and our standard of living will be eroded if we can't stop it. You do understand that," Trunnion coldly stated. There was venom, but it curled away. "It is our world, our universe, and we will fight tooth, claw, and nail to protect it."

"The casino manager. Is it pos—?"

"No," they snapped sharply.

"Died in custody while under interrogation?" It popped out. She hadn't meant to say it, hadn't meant them to hear her cynicism.

"These deaths are unimportant and irrelevant. Today is important, and the fact that you are in charge of the investigation." Whether they gave a smile or a sneer, it was difficult to tell. "Now, you will take all the data, process it, and form your own opinion. Take whatever action is required, and do whatever it takes to apprehend the perpetrators and stop the exodus." Both held her eyes.

"You have our total unanimous support. It is imperative that this is achieved with the utmost speed." This was an order from Arcanum.

"We have chosen you because of your extraordinarily paradoxical mind," Trunnion said. "And your loyalty."

Both men stood, and now there were no smiles. The meeting was at an end, the file was handed to Chapter, and the double doors swung silently open. Chapter left, and the android was waiting for her; this time she didn't pay any attention to the landscape. Her analytical mind was assessing the information she had been given and what her immediate action would be to start the investigation.

Ten

*P*opablu, Dix Dulipper, his naked body a grey-green sheen, emerged like a pupa from the observatory of the *Auriga Lick*, his vision blurred and his throat on fire. He had been woken from his sedated sleep by the voice of Mister Christel urgently commanding him to present himself on the bridge of the ship. He stumbled down the passageways, vaguely aware that other members of his crew were waking and emerging from their sleep cubicles. Someone—he had no idea who—covered him with a dressing gown.

Tall, armoured Sturm police with their ridiculous straw boaters, which were said to be made out of spun steel, were stationed at every intersection. They wore black, sinister suits, shirts, and ties. Their eyes, shaded by wrap-around sunglasses, were staring blankly at him as he crawled past them. He didn't question why they were there or from where they had come. Dix gulped, and tears of fear began to fill his eyes. Soft, terrified mewing filled his ears, and he wondered who it was until he realised it was coming from him. He tried to stifle it, but the mewing resisted and continued until he was outside the door to the bridge. With effort he sucked in a deep breath, expanding his rib cage and counting to ten before releasing it. The screechy mewing stopped, and one of the Sturm police made a signal for the door to open. Dix stepped inside, and the door closed with a jarring clonk, emphasising the cold, heavy silence in the room.

Opposite him, next to Mister Christel, was a tall, elegantly dressed woman in a peak white suit, the harsh overhead lights shining through her silver wire hair and making an intended halo. Her disapproving, satin bronze eyes locked onto his.

"Dix Dulliper?" she stated as though crossing another name off a list.

He tried to say yes, but the word caught in his burning throat, and he nodded.

"Great grandson of Dix Dulipper Borradox?" It was stated with no glowing admiration.

He again tried to speak, and again his throat barred any speech. He squeezed at his throat, and mucus slithered out of his nose.

"I need him to answer verbally." It was an order, and Mister Christel moved quickly away.

"Now, shall we continue this interview, or wait?" She didn't wait. "You have been in travel sedation for two calendars, programmed for three. Because your sedation was interrupted, your bodily functions, physically and mentally, are impaired. Physically you will return to normal within two or three hours, with mental restoration in twenty or thirty minutes. I would prefer it not to take that long." Another command. "Mister Christel."

Mister Christel returned with a phial of liquid, and he made Dix sip slowly from it, holding his nose and tilting his head back. The liquid trickled into his throat.

"Sodium pethidine," the woman announced, watching Mister Christel continue to administer the liquid till the phial was empty. "Now, Mister Christel, I need him compos mentis immediately." She waved her hand at him, and Mister Christel nodded and obeyed the order, moving quickly away.

Detective Inspector Chapter Editor stared at the man standing in front of her. She had no feelings for or against him; she was totally ambivalent. When he answered her questions, he would either condemn or acquit himself. The fact that he was shivering and had mucus running out of his nose, that his eyes held shimmering tears, and that the gown he was wearing emphasised his sallow green nakedness was totally irrelevant to her. He could be putting on an innocent act and be guilty or vice versa; his present body language had no relevant communication, because she already knew he was scared.

The investigation that had brought her onto the bridge of the *Auriga Lick* had been relatively simple. The space navigator's log books and charts had given her the precise location and exact time of when the transmission had been received. An explanation was given regarding the broadcasting nature of this ancient equipment. Varying electrical signals are amplified and used to modulate a carrier wave; the modulated carrier is fed to an antenna, where it is converted to electromagnetic waves, and these waves are sensed by other antennas connected to other receivers. The radius of the amplified electrical signals had been used to select the area to investigate. All spacecrafts travelling in this area had been located, and all of them except two were rejected because of their modern, digital data transmitting systems. The other two were in the *Auriga Lick's* class of spacecraft, with ancient analogue transmission systems, receiving antennas, and modems.

The first craft Detective Chapter Editor had boarded had had the system upgraded to digital, the old-fashioned equipment and transmission abilities destroyed.

That left *Auriga Lick*, plate number five zero zero nine three.

It could have also been a possibility that the signal had been circulating through the galaxy for many years and had only recently been picked up. An inner sense had given Chapter the feeling that she was on the right track. She smelt it, although her rational self dismissed such irrational emotions. If she was right, she had to find out why, where, and for what reason the transmission was made.

A troupe of Candle Dancers, of vaudeville artists, didn't seem to be the right calibre for subversives and terrorists. But the man—the boy— snivelling in front of her had alerted her suspicions.

Mister Christel moved back to Dix and put his hands on his head, moving it over to one side and then the other. Then Christel gently tapped with two fingers on the neck to select a vein, holding a finger against it while he chose a hypodermic syringe from off the steel trolley he had brought with him. He connected a bright shiny standard bevel needle to the syringe before spreading and stretching the skin with his finger and thumb. In a flash of light he quickly stabbed the sharp, hollow needle into the tender, waxy skin, squeezing the plunger fully down before quickly removing it with a flick of his wrist, leaving a small globular of red blood.

Dix had offered no objection; he seemed incapable of any resistance. After the injection Mister Christel briefly applied pressure onto the wound to staunch the blood, and then stepped back to the side of Chapter. They both watched as the injection began to work.

Dix's eyes opened wide; his shrivelled green skin stretched taut, with a pinkish hue seeping back into it. He snorted, drew the mucous back up his nose, swallowed, and released a long and deep breath. "Thank you," he gargled quietly while smiling nervously.

Chapter folded her arms, the halo tilted forward. "Terrorist actions are always related to the ultimate goal of producing political change."

Dix blinked, and his mouth dropped open. Her words made him confused, and he started to blush. The scratching light from the halo hurt his eyes, and he tried to close them but found he couldn't.

"You are Dix Dulipper, stage name Popablu, great grandson of Dix Dulipper Borradox." She watched him has he slowly nodded.

"And you killed, or—" She waited a beat for it to register in his eyes. "Or to be factually correct, you had him killed. The rightful and lawful captain of this ship, Dix Dulipper Dannering. Did you not?" She didn't wait for an answer or acknowledge the slow shaking of Dix Dulipper's head. "We have your co-conspirator, who confirms that it was he who physically killed the Impresario Dix Dulipper Dannering." She unfolded her arms, and her white silk blouse billowed slightly. She waved her hand over a sensor on the consul, the door opened, and Strid Docker, the casino's manager, was thrust forward. Dix glanced at him but didn't show any recognition. "You will confirm that you admitted killing Dix Dannering with a blow to his head."

Docker looked terrified, and his piggy eyes were stretched wide. His mouth sagged open as he slowly nodded his large head and gargled, "Yus."

"In your statement of defence, you gave the reason for this aggressive act, which was that he had his accused you of attempting to solicit the sexual favours of one of the female members of this troupe." She tilted her head slightly, and the halo shimmered. "Correct, Mr. Docker?"

"C-correct," Docker simpered.

"We accept the first part in your statement of defence, that you ended the life of Dix Dulipper Dannering by unlawful means. But we consider the second part of your defence to be a fabrication of lies to protect yourself and an accomplice. This accomplice is the one you are now standing next to?"

Docker turned to briefly look at Dix and then back at Chapter. "Never seen him before." His voice held the tremor of submissive fear.

"You had the man, Dix Dulipper Dannering, killed," Editor said, coldly addressing Popablu and ignoring Docker's answer, "so that you could take over this ship and the Troupe of Candle Dancers for your own political agenda." Her eyes held on Popablu's for a moment. "You wished, by this action, to destabilize the state for totally selfish, egotistical reasons. To destroy your parentage and your kindred blood, which included your uncles Trunnion and Arcanum Bix Bieder." Popablu gulped in astonishment, unable to understand the words he was hearing. "You did this out of malice, because you thought you deserved more respect and more power." She pulled back her shoulders to ease her bra strap; she wanted to do it with her hands, but thought at this stage of the interrogation it would be inappropriate. "You committed this heinous crime with no regard to the consequences." Chapter paused briefly. "You can answer."

Chapter waved her hand over the sensor panel, the door opened, and Chapter signalled that she had finished with Docker. A Sturm guard spun Docker round and roughly pushed him out, and the door closed quietly behind them.

Dix, Popablu looked at her stupefied, the green sheen of the pupa had returned; he had no comprehension of what she was talking about, and he had no answer except to blink.

"We have the transmission which the Android, named Mister Christel, intercepted. It was being transmitted from this ship, the *Auriga Lick*, and I believe it was you and perhaps other accomplices who organised and created this transmission. Correct?"

Popablu's stupefied brain was gradually clearing. Her torrent of words and accusations were being assimilated, and intrinsic chromosomes and genes began to stumble nervously into his brain. *How dare this woman speak to you like this*, a thought, formed from upbringing and breeding, challenged. His eyes flashed silver, burning away the soft grey dullness. "My name is Dix Dulipper Boradox, great grandson of the legendary Dix Dulipper Borradox. My uncles Trunnion Bix Bieder and Arcanum Bix Bieder are the supreme rulers of these worlds and planets; they are the law, and as they are, so I am." His courage, his inherited superiority, had returned. "You invade my ship, and you accuse me of an heinous crimes against my kith and kin. I want an immediate explanation for these fucking lies and accusations. Who the fuck are you, that dare accuse me?" The pupa had transformed into a spitting, poisonous tsetse fly.

Chapter felt the chill of absolute power. Had she misplayed her hand? She had made the assumption that this Dix Bieder was a usurper wishing to take control of the empire. He was the fifth in line and as such would have no chance of inheriting the total supreme position, unless he chose to do it by unlawful action. This was Chapter's original assumption after she had received all the relevant and pertinent information. Taking over the command of the ship after the rightful captain had been killed. Killed by an accomplice, likely to have been offered a position and power when the coup d'état had been achieved. Taking over despite the fact that a man named Estoppel Xit was the rightful successor. Taking over because this allowed him to transmit the image of a new world that was causing the exodus of the workers from the towns and cities, making the current rulers unstable and vulnerable to outside forces. It had all seemed plausible.

But only an assumption, Chapter reminded herself, and without any direct evidence it would remain just that. *Consider your assumptions, but never allow them to be the main plank of your investigations. Only hard facts and inconvertible proof will get you the correct, lawful result.* She remembered an early lecture at the police academy many moons ago. She brushed her hair back and pulled her shoulders upright, and the halo disappeared. *How can this despicable, spoilt brat turd dare to challenge me?* She decided to attack.

"I, Detective Inspector Chapter Editor, hold the full authority of the GEC council and the personal authorisation of Trunnion and Arcanum Bix Bieder to pursue my investigations without hindrance or malice." She waited for this to sink in. "If I choose to have you arrested now, have you interned, and have the command of this ship taken from you, I would have their total backing." Her nostrils flared. "So shut the fuck up and answer only the questions that I ask you." She stared into the flashing silver eyes and watched the red blush burn across his soft, boyish face. "Where did you obtain the images of this new world?" She waited a moment for an answer but saw only amazement and bewilderment in his eyes. "Have you visited it? And if so, why don't your logs or navigational readouts record any divergence from your scheduled flight path?" Still there only bewilderment. "Or have they been tampered with? Answer."

She watched his eyes for signs of a lie; if they flicked up to the right this was a sign that he might be considering lying. There was no movement, and his now dulled, lifeless grey eyes stared straight ahead.

"Did you understand the questions?" she asked, watching his mouth sag open and the slow shake of his head. She was about to continue when he began to speak slowly and clearly.

"I have not a fucking clue what you are talking about." His eyes flashed.

"No?" She nodded at Mister Christel, who stepped over to a bank of monitors and flicked a switch. The monitor screens shimmered briefly, and then the scenes of the new world appeared. Chapter's eyes never left Popablu's, and she knew as he watched the scenes being played back that he had never ever seen them before. His eyes widened, and a smile of amazement lit his face.

"This is the transmission Mister Christel intercepted."

"It's fantastic, unbelievable," Popablu said. He took his eyes briefly away from the screen. "And this exists?" he asked Chapter, returning his gaze to the screen.

Chapter waited for the images to fade and for Mister Christel to switch the monitors off before replying. "At this moment and from your reaction, I believe that this was the first time you have seen this transmission." Dix nodded. "And you were not aware of, or had any part in the transmission of those scenes?" Dix nodded again. "Those scenes you have just seen are considered to be an act of terrorism against the state. They have already caused a mass exodus from the towns and cities. The work force is being depleted, and this threatens the sustainable life on the world and planets. In believing that you are now innocent, I request—I command you to assist in tracking down the perpetrators of this action."

"That was amazing," exclaimed Dix, still entranced by the images he had seen.

"Yes, and they were transmitted from this ship. How, why, and by whom, I intend to find out. It is vital for the security and survival of the worlds that I get this information as quickly as possible. Have you any knowledge of subversives within your troupe who would want to usurp our leaders or destabilise our society?"

Dix pursed his lips and thought for a moment, and then shook his head. "No." He was going to say sorry but decided not to apologise to the bitch.

Chapter looked away from him as the door hummed open for a Sturm troop Captain to enter. "Yes, Captain?" She hoped he was going to give her good news.

"We have interviewed the crew and most of the troupe, and—"

Chapter interrupted. "Most of?"

"Four haven't been accounted for. We have been informed that they are thought to be hiding somewhere in the bowels of the ship."

"Did you find out why they are in hiding?"

Popablu gave a screech in between a laugh and a cry before the captain could reply. "Deeks," he squealed. "They stole his body and took it away."

"Deeks?" queried Chapter.

"Dix Dannering, the governor." He hesitated as though trying to remember. "Who that that Docker killed. They took it because they didn't believe he was dead. Oh my . . ." His voice trailed off and his mouth stayed open.

"These four are?" She looked at the captain.

He referred to his electronic recorder. "Babe Algol, Estoppel Xit, Jollity Strad, and Irma Iggy."

She turned back to look hard at Dix and said sharply. "These are the four who stole the body?"

Dix nodded and then whispered, "I think, yes. They haven't been seen since."

"They believed he was alive, although you considered him dead?" Chapter asked.

"Yes, no. No, I didn't," Dix stammered. "The scanners, the life support systems pronounced him dead, and Mister Christel." He pointed vigorously at Mister Christel.

"The clinical administrator?"

"Medial officer," corrected Popablu. "They have the final affirmation."

"Yes." Chapter said. She briefly paused to study Popablu for a moment. "So Dix Dannering was dead, and his body was stolen from . . . ?" She looked at Mister Christel.

"The medical bay," Mister Christel answered.

"And taken to some place in the bowels of this craft?" Mister Christel nodded, and Chapter looked back at Popablu accusingly. "A violation of the galactic laws. Why did you not apprehend these people? Why did you allow them this freedom?"

"I didn't consider it necessary at the time. They had nowhere to go. There would have been time when we docked at our next port." Dix answered hurriedly.

"Ummh," Chapter murmured. She looked away from Popablu. A thought, an assumption was forming in her mind, but at the moment it was only that. She issued a sharp command to the Captain. "Locate the position of the four, and let me know immediately. Don't accost them. I will want to interview them in situ."

"Fuck, you think it's them?" Popablu uttered, and then he gave a surprised gasp as thoughts twisted through his brain. *Why did that man Docker confess to killing Dannering, when he must have known it was me who killed him, me who squeezed the life out of him while pretending to staunch the flow of blood? He was there, standing behind me, but he kept quiet. Why did he keep quiet? He must have known who I was, known that I was connected, and wants recompense for his silence. Fucking amazing. He confessed, and I'm now totally in the clear. The fool.* His thoughts were interrupted by a woman he hadn't noticed before moving from behind him to the detective and whispering to her.

Chapter smiled. From the moment she had suspected the involvement of the personnel on the spacecraft *Auriga Lick*, she had requested the services of the android programmed with the ability of thought transference. The information she was now being given was provoking but at the moment was of no consequence. She believed that the Dix in front of her wasn't responsibility for the transmission. This was her priority; the murder could wait. She thanked the android and smiled at Dix, but the smile held no humour. However, she totally believed that this boy in front of her had never seen the transmission before. He was a Candle Dancer, an actor, and actors could create emotions; they had a repertoire of behavioural techniques, to make people believe in them. *Had he just done that?* she asked herself, and she decided to hold judgement until the missing four had been found. The Sturm police with their sensors shouldn't take long.

Dix Dannering woke. He was being shaken gently by Xit. "What?" he asked

"We have visitors." Xit's voice trembled slightly.

Dix sat up. Walking towards him was a tall woman with bright silver hair dressed in a shining white suit. Dix thought she was the most beautiful woman he had seen in his whole life. At first he didn't notice the armed, black suited men in boaters who followed her.

"You're supposed to be dead." To Dix her voice sounded musical, magical; it also had the wonderful timbre of humour held in it.

"Yes I suppose I should," Dix answered, laughing, standing up, and extending his hand to her. When she gave him hers, he raised it to his lips and kissed it before releasing it.

"Did you transmit scenes of a new world?" Her face was beautiful, and her soft satin burnished eyes sparkled with laughter.

"A new world?" Dix queried, and then realised she meant the sets and scenery he had transmitted for Popablu to receive. "Yes, yes," he said happily. "We sent them to show Popablu what show business should be about. It was something that he would never be able to achieve in a million years."

Then he noticed Popablu cowering amongst the armed men, his face drained of blood with the sheen of a dead fish. The boy looked very nervous, as though he had seen a ghost.

"Oh dear," Dix said quietly. "I don't think you are here to pay me a compliment."

He looked into the beautiful eyes and felt an overwhelming desire to kiss her and swing her round and round. Dix Dannering had fallen in love. Love at first sight was something he would never have believed possible.

"Why did you do it?" the sweetest voice in the whole universe asked.

"To show him he could never be as good as the old school. He didn't have the background or training."

"Let me introduce myself," she said. Dix smiled and nodded. "Detective Inspector Chapter Editor. I am here to arrest the perpetrators of the transmitted images, which have caused and are causing havoc amongst the population of our worlds."

Dix sat down like a puppet when the strings have gone slack. His jaw dropped down in total amazement. "The world, havoc?" he squeaked.

"You admit to it?"

"No, no, it couldn't be. It was an internal transmission only for him," he muttered. "Only for him." He waved a finger in the direction of Popablu.

"I want you to explain to me how you obtained the transmitted scenes. Did you get them from a new world, a new planet that you have discovered?" Her soft gentle voice had Dix captivated, and he couldn't help smiling and gazing into her eyes.

"Discovered a new world? No, we made it—us." He held his hand out towards the other four. "It came from the old world." He was pleased with his response. "I know it shouldn't have, and I should have destroyed it all, but I didn't, I couldn't. I kept everything. You have seen it, you have seen how beautiful it is. How could one destroy it?"

Chapter was becoming slightly bemused. She had instantly liked this man—his pale green eyes ringed with orange, his shiny bald head, his wonderful and innocent smile. She couldn't accept that he was the leader of terrorists who threatened to destabilise and destroy society. But he had admitted that he had transmitted the images. "You made it?" she asked incredulously.

"Well sort of," replied Dix. "We didn't paint the cloths or scrims or build the sets; they were done in my father's time. No, we brought them out of retirement from the holds, where they had been hidden for years. We hung the cloths, erected the scaffold and sets, built the grid, and hung the lights." He gestured with hands up to the roof. "I suppose we did make the water effect, which was . . ."

Chapter held up her hand to stop him speaking. *A beautiful gesture,* thought Dix. How he longed to brush it with kisses. "And you made a recording of it, which you transmitted. After that, did you destroy the cloths and sets?"

"Destroy them?" Dix laughed. "Of course not! Why would anyone want to destroy them? They're beautiful, priceless. Only . . ." he was going to say, "Only idiotic, despotic rulers would do that." But he stopped himself as he saw out of the corner of his eye a Sturm trooper scratching his nose. He returned his attention to the enchanting face. "I can show you them if you like," he said, standing up and turning. Then he stopped. "Oh, if I'm allowed to. Am I under arrest?"

"I would like to see them." Chapter was feeling unsure of herself. She had made up her mind that he wasn't a terrorist, that he hadn't attempted to destabilise society, that the whole situation was a terrible mistake, an attempt to show off that had gone horribly wrong. Childish it may be, but not a premeditated act of political violence.

"Certainly, certainly. Please follow us." He waved his hands at the other four to signal them to move, which they did hesitantly and reluctantly at first, moving towards a pair of huge doors. Jollity reached them first and swung them open. Xit, Irma, and Babe ran and waddled through them and disappeared into the dark void. Dix, followed by Chapter, the Sturm troopers and Popablu, entered through the doors into the darkness of a large, cavernous room. The Sturm Troopers quietly unlocked the safety catches on their weapons and held them at the ready.

"Sorry it's a little dark. Xit will switch on a working light, and then we'll be—Ah, good." A small faint light glowed. "Please follow me. Keep close." He sensed rather than felt Chapter moving closer to him, and he wanted to reach out and take her hand but resisted the impulse.

"We have arrived at the back of the set," he said it in a reverential whisper. "I will take you round and find you a suitable place to stand so that you can see the glory of it." He gave a slight, depreciating laugh. Everyone followed, peering into the soft mushroom-coloured gloom; it was very difficult to see anything.

If this is a trap, an ambush, then it is being conducted in a very charming way. Chapter thought to herself as she sensed the nervousness of the Sturm troopers.

"We've arrived," said Dix, stopping. "Now, if you can all gather together in a little group, you'll get the full magnificence of it all." He gave another giggle. "We had to adapt the lighting to make it work from the ship's magna power; at the first moment when it trips on, it is very bright, so I suggest that when I clap my hands, you cover your eyes for a moment, and on the second clap you can uncover them."

"Ma'am." the Sturm captain stepped up to Chapter. "I can't allow that."

"Of course not, Captain. Do your men have solar protectors?" The Captain nodded. "I suggest they wear them."

"Yes, ma'am." The captain stepped back and issued an order to his men. The Sturm troopers took the optical devices, which were black strips of soft glass, from the pockets of their coats and exchanged them for their wrap-arounds, putting them over their eyes.

"Okay?" Dix said. "It will take a few moments before the lamps have warmed up. I will still do the claps, first one to shield your eyes, second one to look."

Everyone was standing very still and tense, and nervous breathing drummed into the silence. Dix wished he could feel her breath but resisted moving any closer to her.

"All set." Xit's shout pierced the breathing.

"Go." Dix shouted back, at the same time clapping his hands together.

Chapter lifted her hands to her eyes, praying that she hadn't been led into a trap by this strangely attractive man. She held her breath, her eyes tightly closed, willing the second clap to come quickly.

The Sturm troopers cowered back as a dazzling, bright light burnt out the room as though a star had exploded. Their black glasses reflected the pure white solar light, and all closed their eyes instantly.

When the second clap came, it exploded like a thunderclap and echoed into every corner of the vast space.

All eyes shot open, hands dropped away from faces, and glasses were slipped off. The collective gasp at the scene in front of them resounded louder than a thunder clap. They were all there, magically transported into the new world. It was unbelievable, as though they had stepped into a dream. They felt detached from reality; all belief in reality had been suspended.

One of the Sturm troopers ran forward to the sea and was about to touch it when a sharp cry from Dix stopped him. "It's mercury—deadly poisonous." Dix moved to him and gently ushered him away.

"Mercury?" Chapter asked with amazement, looking at the tantalising, glittering sea that lapped in front her.

"Mercury," Dix said, moving close to Chapter. Her skin was like the white apple blossom painted on the scenic cloth. "From the soil tanks.

It was the only thing we could think of. In the old days it would have been water skimmed over sheets of mirror. But that's quite effective, don't you think?" The smell of her perfume washed over him.

"Very," Chapter said enthusiastically. "Very effective." Her brain held a small, lingering doubt, still unsure that her eyes had been deceived by the created effect, that it wasn't for real. "And the fountains?" she asked, feeling like a small girl asking stupid questions.

"Oh, they are just cut cloths with flicker lights fluttering behind them," he said dismissively.

"Very impressive, though they look real, with the water rising and falling." She felt herself blushing at her gauche enthusiasm.

"Inkies and flutter lights on chasers give the sparkle and ripple effect." He pointed at the small lights round the edge of the set. "The azure blue is created by the two ks, two kilowatts lamps above you; one has a cobalt gel, the other turquoise. The slowly revolving disc clamped onto the barn doors helps the impression that the sea is undulating." He watched her as she looked up above. Her slender neck could have been sculpted out of pink alabaster, and he wondered how many kisses it would take from shoulders to head. She looked back down at the set, her eyes were wide, bright and sparkling. "Two brutes, and this is normally not done." When he saw that she didn't understand the terminology, he quickly explained. "Brutes are enormously powerful ten-kilowatt lights with fresnel lenses set at the back of the cloth, to shine through it, help the dimension, increase the luminance. The . . ." He stopped suddenly and smiled coyly. "Sorry, I'm getting carried away—too technical."

"No, no it's fascinating." Golden sunlight was flickering through the lattice work, and Chapter located the lights that were creating this effect. "Fascinating." Then she thought to herself, *All just an illusion, a simple illusion that has created havoc, mayhem, and frustration for the brothers Trunnion and Arcanum.*

Dix interrupted her thinking. "We recorded it all on these old cameras." He ran a finger down the side of his nostril and placed it on the lens. "The slightest grease round the lens to soften the focus."

"There were other scenes?" Chapter queried, remembering the transmission.

"Yes, six. I can show you them if you have the time. This one will be de-rigged and another one erected. It takes about a week."

"A week?" Chapter wasn't really listening to him; she was trying to decide what her next move would be. She was vaguely aware of Dix enthusiastically saying they could try to do it quicker, but there was only the five of them. She finally made up her mind. She would have to arrest them, but she reconsidered: all five, or just him? Just him, she decided. The others would stay on the *Auriga Lick* under guard, and she would take him back with her to show the brothers their evil protagonist.

She felt elated that she had made a decision, and then made another more important decision. *I will make love to him first.* She felt even more elated. She had decided to do this from the first moment she had seen him, from the first moment when she had entered the bowels of the ship where the Sturm troopers had located them and had informed her. "We have located five persons at map reference—."

"Five?" Chapter had queried, interrupting the location explanation.

"Four as named before, and a Dix Dannering—the one presumed deceased."

"He's alive?"

"Affirmative."

She didn't question why she felt so much love for him. She was unaccountably overwhelmed by it. He was an enemy of the state, a dangerous terrorist whom she had been given the task of tracking down and bringing to justice. He should have been ugly, arrogant in his malevolence, a cornered cur spitting and scratching. Not beautiful, not handsome, not gracious.

She had witnessed in his face, in his voice, his immediate love of her. It had unnerved her for a split, finite second, and then she had laughed—not a physical laugh that showed on her face. She had laughed inside herself, inside her heart, because she knew that she loved him. It seemed silly. She suspected that men fell in love quickly and easily from the sheer physical presence of a woman; an ancient, primeval instinct was instilled in them to have mates to whom they were physically and instantly attracted. Perhaps this was from the hunter's instinct; they didn't have time for consideration or deliberation, which were used only in the stalking and hunting of food.

"I have to kill the lights or they'll burn out. Will that be all right?" Dix asked. His voice was nervously formal.

"Yes, of course," she said, conscious that even in this simple reply she displayed her love for him.

"If you leave first, you will be able to see your way out," It was gentle, simple, courtesy.

"Thank you." Instinctively, after years of police training, she called the captain over. "We are going to leave now. You and a few of your men will stay here to accompany Mr. Dix and the others out after the lights are turned off." Instantly she felt guilty. She had seen Dix blink as she was giving the order, and she knew that he felt betrayed, as if she didn't trust him.

He smiled weakly and sadly. She wanted to wrap her arms round him, hold him and apologise, and kiss his watery eyes. But instead she moved with the others away from the set and into the outer bay, hoping that he would understand that it was a part she had to play so that no one would suspect their love of each other.

"Kill the lights," she heard Dix yell. Was there hurt in his voice? She couldn't tell. The room behind her was instantly plunged into darkness; the lights hissed and crackled for a moment, and then there was dead silence.

Eleven

.

*T*he walls and floors of the interview room were tiled in white vermiculated blocks to absorb sound, but they allowed the transference of thoughts. The lights in an opaque glass ceiling dismissed shadows and shapes but couldn't banish the heavy, dark circles around Dix's eyes. From the observation window, Chapter, the transfer of thoughts android, and the brothers Trunnion and Arcanum stared down at Dix. They didn't want intimacy with the prisoner, their enemy.

"What's he thinking?" Trunnion asked the android.

"Patterns," she answered simply.

"Patterns?" queried Trunnion.

"Coloured patterns."

"Nothing else?"

"Nothing else."

"He's cleverer than you think," Arcanum said, smiling at the reflection of Chapter in the observation room's dark glass windows.

Chapter stared down at the shiny bald head and wished she could again cover it in wild, abandoned kisses. She wanted to hold him again, to run the tips of her fingers over his lips, to feel his naked body next to hers.

"I believe he is very clever," Chapter replied, feeling Arcanum's eyes forensically examining her face in the dark reflection, hoping that it didn't betray her love of Dix.

"We aren't achieving anything by this," Trunnion said impatiently.

"A few more days may produce something," answered Arcanum, still investigating Chapter's reflection. "And you still believe that it was an accident, created to prove professional superiority?"

Chapter nodded. She had given the explanation the day she had returned with Dix, knowing that they wouldn't believe her, or wouldn't want to believe her. They wanted an act of political terrorism, something they could repress and root out the perpetrators and execute them. This was what they could understand and deal with—not some silly theatrical boasting that accidentally got out of hand.

If she could have persuaded them to meet him, they perhaps might have accepted the simple explanation and the simple fact that he was innocent. But they were adamant and refused to even contemplate a face-to-face meeting. He was their enemy, a terrorist with aims of self-interest and illogical destructiveness of the state, attempting to remove the structural supports that gave them their strength and domination. They wanted to know how and why it had been possible for him to create such mayhem, how their repression and mass coercion had been resisted. This was the only reason that he had been allowed to live.

Chapter had persuaded them that she could prove his innocence, but they were becoming impatient and wanted a result that they believed in, and they wanted it fast. The Sturm interviewers had been alerted.

Chapter wanted to hold Dix like she had on the night he came to her, after he had disappeared the second time. She remembered that moment again.

Someone had started to sing, a beautiful and simple sound with notes held long and clear, a boy's voice. Chapter had shivered and had wondered how a boy came to be down in the bowels of the *Auriga Lick*.

Dix was leading, and in the line behind him was Babe Algol, Irma, Jollity, and then Estoppel Xit. It was Xit who was singing. At first Chapter thought it was impossible; it couldn't be the old, decrepit cripple. But his mouth was opening and closing, and the beautiful notes were coming from it. The woman called Irma was dancing in and out of the line, round it and through it, and spinning gracefully up over their heads.

They had emerged through the large doors, and the captain and six of his men followed, attentively watching the flash of white pants as the girl's skirt spiralled round her as she danced and flew. It was magical. The five formed a circle and spun round faster and faster. The woman Irma appeared like a beautiful candle in the centre and seemed to spin upwards, her skirt spreading out over the other four spinning below, and her long, slender legs cork-screwing and winding her upwards. At the top the brilliant white flashed, holding the focus of everyone in the room. Suddenly the singing stopped, silence filled the area, and Irma slid down and curled onto the floor. Instant applause erupted. The captain and his men were smiling, and Chapter was laughing and clapping. This eventually came to faltering to a stop as they gazed at the group fazed. They were unable to believe their eyes; there was only four of them.

Chapter counted and recounted. Irma the dancer, Xit the singer, Babe Agol, and one called Jollity were still there. Four, not five.

Chapter swore under her breath. She'd been duped! She thought he had loved her. Dix Dannering, the main perpetrator, had disappeared. It was impossible. How could he disappear before everyone's eyes?

She immediately ordered a search but knew it would be unsuccessful. Everyone was ordered to return to their quarters. The betrayer of her trust and love would eventually be found even if she had to take the ship apart plate by plate, she had stated to the captain.

The android, Mister Christel, had suggested that her quarters could be the observation globe, which she quietly accepted.

It had taken her a long time to finally fall asleep. She should have felt annoyed that she'd been betrayed, but in fact she didn't feel betrayed—she felt amused, and her amusement was what was annoying her. She was amused that a man had duped her with a simple theatrical trick, the trick of distraction. *Now you see it, now you don't.* Her father had shown her many card tricks and had shown her how to make a distraction with one hand while slipping cards away with the other. This had been his downfall—he had been caught doing it while playing cards professionally in a big card game. Her father, whom she loved more than anything and anyone in the universe, was outlawed and branded as a cheat and a liar. She let the thought drift away . . .

And now she had fallen in love with another man who was brilliant at the art of allusion and distraction. What would his fate be? She didn't want to consider the answer.

She heard her name being softly sung. "Chapter." She had been dreaming of being pushed on a swing by her father, a swing that creaked and groaned as she swung backwards and forwards, high into the glass dome of their home. "Chapter," the voice whispered. Her heart fluttered in her chest, and the swing began slowing down. On the next swing of the pendulum she decided to jump. Perhaps she had been too high, because she was flying, somersaulting over and over into waking, unsure of where she was as her eyes flickered open. A soft, velvet "You are beautiful." breathed and caressed her ear. She turned her head, and he was there, Dix, lying next to her.

"How?" she whispered. "The guards . . . ?"

"I got here before them, before you." His eyes twinkled in the darkness.

She squirmed round on the sleeping couch, placed her hand on his face, and smiled. "The master illusionist." Then she kissed him. He slipped his arms round her back and gently pulled her closer into him, and she felt his penis stiffening as he was kissing her and she was kissing him. They slipped their clothes off, skin touching, the most beautiful moment in time. He felt her teeth, took her tongue, and was inside her making love, each whispering the other's name softly, over and over.

"You will have to take me back," he finally whispered, gently kissing her neck after each word.

"No, no," she gasped. "We can disappear."

"They will find us."

Then she had gone silent knowing that he was right, knowing that they couldn't escape or hide away, knowing that she would have to hand him over to the brothers. She would have to use all her wits, every participle of her intelligence and her persuasion, to keep him alive.

Tears glistened in her eyes.

"Before you introduce your captured terrorist to the brothers," he said, softly interrupting her thoughts as he licked the shiny pearl tears from her eyes, "I would like to take you somewhere very special, very beautiful, it wouldn't take long, a small detour; we would hardly be missed."

"Where?" She heard the hint of wary accusation in her voice.

He had held a finger against her lips. "It's not a trick, promise. I won't disappear." His eyes sparkled with laughter. "It will be my gift to you, for you to remember and hold this moment."

"Where?" she asked again, this time excited by this beautiful, strange man who lay beside her. She was excited by his mystery and his love. A shooting star briefly illuminated the sphere and brought with it a sharp, brilliant white reality that shot through Chapter. "The brothers—you know them?" The harshness of her question felt alien, and she pulled him closer into her.

"Arcanum and Trunnion are truly the greatest showmen of the galaxy. Their stage is all the planets, and we are merely actors who do their bidding, accepting their direction no matter how bad we think it is, because we have—"

"No alternative." Chapter squeezed even closer to him and kissed him. Her tongue pressed and rolled round his tongue, biting and teasing it.

"No, balls," he gasped out, laughing as she released him from the devouring kiss.

He gently moved across her and sat up, gazing into her eyes. She felt the gaze penetrate her mind, her thoughts, and it made her smile. All her thoughts were of him and how much she loved him; it was total, overwhelming, hypnotic. She felt his fingers stroking her like a soft breath touching every part of her, every hollow, every indentation.

"For you," he whispered. He blinked, releasing her from his gaze.

She looked down between her breast and was amazed to see that he was holding a bunch of snowy white flowers. "They are beautiful! Where . . . ?" She reached out, but before her finger tips reached them they had disappeared. She looked at him, and he smiled down at her and blew her a kiss.

"And for you." He looked away to where the flowers had been, and she followed his look and gasped. Sitting in place of the flowers was a white animal with long ears and its nose twitching. Chapter laughed.

"And again for you." He bent down and kissed her nose, and then he sat upright. He was holding a white turtle dove, fluttering in his hands. With a slight movement he threw it upwards, and the dove flew high above them into the bowl of velvet darkness before disappearing.

Chapter sat up, her mouth still open in amazement, her head tilted back and still looking after the dove. "How? Where did they . . . ? Where did you get them from?"

"Ah, a professional magician never reveals his secrets." He held a finger to her lips. "But for you, I shall have no secrets. The bouquet of flowers."

He took his fingers away from her lips and quickly wrapped and twisted them into the white sheet, his other hand quickly fanning and flicking out the shapes of the petals. Chapter laughed and applauded, and then she cheered even more enthusiastically as the flowers dissolved into the white sheet and the white rabbit appeared, its nose twitching as before. Briefly Dix twisted it round so that she could see that it was his fingers that were making the twitching nose. Then he spread his hands to allow the sheet to float back across Chapter's hips.

"The dove—show me the dove." She felt like a child again, trapped and held with the mystery and magic of allusions.

"That had to be real?" He smiled, his eyes sparkling with mischief.

"Show me." She smiled back at him, pouting and blowing a kiss of disbelief.

"You don't believe me?" he asked in a small boy's hurt voice. His eyes held hers.

"How could it fly?"

Out of the corner of her eye, she saw another fluttering white shape, another turtle dove. She turned to look at it, and at the same moment Dix threw it upwards, releasing it out of his hands. This time it didn't soar up into the darkness of the dome but fluttered slowly down onto Chapter's legs, and she gently picked it up. "Mica paper," she whispered, holding it up to her mouth and gently blowing the soft, gossamer-thin paper. The wings fluttered and the dove rose, floating up into the soft, deep black.

They both watched till it had faded away.

"Thermals," Chapter said. "That's how you make them fly."

Dix nodded, taking her hands and whispering kisses onto her fingers.

"That was beautiful, thank you. But perhaps I might want you to keep secrets."

"That the dove was real?" he said, laughing. "You wanted to believe it was real?"

"Perhaps."

"But you couldn't have believed it was real forever. You would have doubts, would have questioned the possibility of the existence of a live turtle dove."

Chapter thought for a moment before answering. "Yes I suppose, and it not being live, I saw beauty in another way." She affectionately stroked his shiny bald head. "Your creations. Thank you for showing me how they were created; that makes them even more beautiful and even more wondrous and amazing."

"To see how something is made, to look behind the scenes, to see how an allusion was created and made to work. Painting, music, sculpture, theatre, politics—these have fascinated me and given me the greatest pleasure." Dix leaned forward and kissed her forehead, her eyes, her lips whispering as he did. "You are even more beautiful, even more wondrous, even more amazing." He took each nipple and gently bit, his fingers caressing her breasts, her stomach, her back, tracing round the triangle. She pulled him closer, helped him slip inside her, making them one, and they made love again and again, as though it was impossible to separate, as though they were fearful of being two again.

They woke. She cradled in his arms her head resting on his chest.

"Time we left," He whispered softly.

"No, please no," she gave a sleepy murmur.

"The ancient light won't last."

She shook her head, pulling him closer to him.

"You must see it, you must hear it. It is more amazing than any magic, more than anything made by man. It is creation and will be our love." Dix kissed her awake.

They left, Chapter tall and upright and issuing sharp commands to the captain, who had made a request that two of his men would accompany the detective inspector in case of any trouble. The request had not been accepted; a sarcastic snort and brief shake of her head had dismissed it as an impertinent suggestion.

Dix had his head bowed, his torso, arms, and hands bound tightly in shiny wire cling threads. He looked neither left nor right, avoiding eye contact with any of his cast or crew, who had been summoned to witness his departure.

Xit attempted to protest but was immediately brutally silenced by a Sturm trooper. This couldn't silence the atmosphere of total loathing that surrounded them as Dix, followed by the android who was shyly smiling, flicking her eyes at Dix and then up to Chapter, entered into the air lock of dull black Sturm trooper's space wagon.

The doors hissed closed, and moments later there was deep, soft booming as the wagon's magnets were reversed, expelling it like a ball bouncing off a wall, away from the side of the *Auriga Lick* and into the deep jet blackness of space.

Chapter had immediately released Dix from the bonds of silver wire, unable to resist kissing him all over his face as she did so. When Dix was free, she started to reset the coordinates to the destination he wanted them to arrive at. This simple task was delayed longer than it needed to be, with both needing to kiss each other; when one attempted to concentrate, the other would gently kiss the neck, the head, the eyes, the hands, arms, ears. They had to stop, both agreed with a giggle.

"Be serious."

"Yes."

"The coordinates first, and then we'll make love."

"Yes, yes."

This agreement was a total failure.

"Make love now and set the coordinates afterwards."

"Yes."

"But," he whispered, brushing an ear. "If we set them now, instantly, we can make love until the time we arrive."

A mutual acknowledgement, and although they were starving and craving for each other, the coordinates were quickly tapped in and the direction was set. By the time the powerful magnets had slightly pivoted and the dull black wagon began to change direction, Dix and Chapter had slipped, pulled, snapped each other's clothes off. They tumbled caressing into the sleeping quarters naked, Dix kissing Chapter's stomach, ribcage, and breasts. By the time the new direction was established, they were making love as though it was the first time.

Many first times came and went till they both fell happily into a deep sleep.

Dix woke to the soft murmuring of Chapter's breaths, his arm cradled round her and his hand cupping her breast. He moved to kiss her perfect lips, wanting to make love again, but then he stopped. The magnets had separated, and they were being held still, suspended in space like a spider held by invisible threads. They had reached their destination. He moved his hand.

"Chapter, we have arrived."

"Mmm?" her arm snaked round him and pulling him in closer.

"My beautiful love." He resisted slightly, swaying gently back and slipping his other arm under her knees. "Come with me." He kneeled and then stood, lifting Chapter up. "You must watch and listen to what we are going to see and hear." He carried her out of the sleeping cavity and up to the wagon's command deck.

"Mmm, Dix, I love you carrying me like a baby."

"My baby, you must wake up now."

Chapter's eyes blinked sleepily open. "Yes?"

"Look out there." He nodded towards the circular window.

Chapter twisted her head. "What, Dix?"

"Shush." He gently kissed the top of her head. "Look."

Chapter gasped in amazement as the cabin of the dull black wagon and their naked bodies were washed in red, purple, blue, and shimmering white showers of exhilarating colours that raced towards the circular window. These colours were interlaced with swirling silver and golden traces. Tiny pearl necklaces the colour of raindrops, softly lucent, danced though them, and sparkling silver, orange, and red fireflies seemed to hover for a second and then were gone.

"It is beautiful." Tears glistened in Chapter's eyes.

Their hearts were beating, and through the soft drumming came a thin, high-pitched note held long and clear. It was followed by another pitched lower, and then more wild, weird, and thrilling music followed. They were exhilarating sounds, each harmonic nuance pitched against a dark, sombre resonance of thunder out of tune and harsh.

Chapter gripped Dix tighter. "What is it?" she asked with a tremor of fear.

"The music of the stars," He said softly, hardly audible.

Chapter breathed in deeply, holding her breath to hear every note, every cadence.

"A star is being born." He said it in a hushed whisper of respect.

Her grip relaxed. "A star? Oh Dix, it is beautiful." She twisted in his arms to kiss him. "You are beautiful."

He held the kiss for a moment and then turned, releasing it, gently keeping his cheek next to hers. Through the circular window the colours and shapes were held as if in a painting, and then they billowed as if a wind had blown into them, but only for a fraction, a blink of an eye, before the colours imploded, swallowed back, twisting and spiralling and fleeing away to a pinpoint in the overwhelming blackness of space. As if on cue, the harmony of the music became discordant, the thunder whimpered, and long notes scratched backwards before fading away to a pounding, empty silence.

Neither breathed, their eyes, hearts, and minds concentrating on the tiny, iridescent pinprick of light.

"It is the best present I have ever been given." Chapter whispered, tears running down her cheeks. "Thank you."

"A newborn star, now probably nearly two thousand years old." Dix laughed.

"Yes," Chapter murmured, knowing the physics of the universe. "But you knew where to look for it. I shall never forget." She kissed him again.

"Don't look at me." The hushed, whispering voice of the android brought Chapter back to the reality of the observation room and the solitary figure of her beloved Dix standing below her. The brothers had moved and were sitting down on the other side of the room, away from her.

"It was very beautiful. You are both very beautiful. It was a privilege for me to listen to love," the android continued whispering. Chapter felt a blush heating her face. She had forgotten that the android had been with them when the star had been born and when they had made love. She thought she should apologise for forgetting about her existence.

"Please don't apologise, but listen. They have reached a decision: he is to be exterminated along with every other troupe of Candle Dancers. I'm sorry," the android said hurriedly.

Chapter gulped back a cry and then commanded herself to think clearly, to dismiss any emotional feelings. She had to find a solution, an answer, and she knew she had little time.

She glanced down at Dix, who turned slightly and lifted his head. His eyes found hers even though she knew he couldn't see her through the mirrored glass. He smiled his soft gentle smile, and his eyes held mischief. In them it gave her the answer, the solution she needed.

She crossed over to the brothers, who looked up sharply as she approached.

"Excuse me," Chapter said, smiling at each of them. "I believe I have an answer to our problem."

"*Our* problem?" Trunnion queried sarcastically, examining his manicured nails.

"Yes." Chapter ignored the sarcasm. "How we stop the belief in the mythical promised land, how we stop the exodus, how we show that it was just a piece of theatrical nonsense, and how foolish it was for anyone to take it seriously, to be taken in by wattle and daub." She had used Dix's disparaging expression for scenery. "We were, I believe, taken in by it. Each of us secretly thought such a place might exist, a land, a world that hadn't been discovered until now. To be honest with you, I did hope it existed; I even dreamt of escaping to it if it was proven to exist. I am sure everyone in the galaxy had the same thoughts, including you two." She didn't wait for a denial. "And you wouldn't be who you are if you haven't already been devising ways of taking over your rightful positions in this new world."

Their faces were impassive. "You have no idea how shattered I was, how stupid and foolish I felt when it was shown to me to be just wattle, just theatrical painted scenery. I did feel cheated and angry." She gave each a look. "Not angry at the allusion or the scenery, but anger at myself for being so stupid, so naïve to believe it when there was no rationale, no evidence scientific or astrological, for such a world to exist."

Chapter paused, and the two brothers were studying her. Their faces remained impassive, and their eyes gave no indication of their thoughts; they were waiting for her to continue.

"How to denigrate this belief is to demonstrate it." Trunnion raised an eyebrow at her idea, but she continued. "Put it on, show it, let people come and see it and observe it. Let Dix Dannering mount a show, a theatrical event in a number one theatre with all the props, the scenery, the acts. Let it be seen as visual fallacy, theatrical deception." She felt exhilarated, and her heart pounded against her rib cage. "An event like that has not been seen for years. The whole spectacle will convince people of their stupidity, and the power of this statement will spread like wildfire by word of mouth. The exodus to the mythical promised land will stop."

Chapter was vaguely aware that behind her, the android had given a cry and then had crumpled onto the floor. She hadn't seen the brothers make any movement or give any command, but doors had glided open and Sturm guards had entered from both directions. The brothers rose simultaneously from their chairs.

Chapter felt a dull blow to the back of her knees, and she folded to the floor. She felt the sharp pinprick of pain in the back of her neck and knew a syringe had been used; in a few seconds she was unconscious. In those few winking seconds she glimpsed the highly polished black shoes of the brothers head towards her and stand for a beat before moving away. She thought she heard Trunnion hiss coldly and acidly, "Your assignment was to deliver the perpetrators, not to fall in love." But she couldn't be sure, and darkness folded and coiled round her.

Twelve

A sharp, stinging pain brought Chapter awake, and she had a blurred awareness that she was stretched face down across a cold-topped table. A painful metal edge dug into her hips, her arms were pulled above her head with hands held tight, her breasts were squashed flat on the cold hard surface, and her feet were locked together onto the floor. The stinging, burning red pain was coming from her buttocks, and she knew she had been caned.

A voice behind murmured, and she felt fingers gently stroking along the stripes of pain. "Good, the skin isn't broken; there will be bruising." She felt ointment being smeared over her buttocks. "But not for long."

The pain began to subside, and her awareness focused and became sharp. The nasal voice continued. "A caning of the buttocks never did anyone any harm. A recalcitrant wife or mistress, eh?" A rhetorical question—no answer was expected. "When released she'll be a little unsteady. The injection and the caning." The voice was distracted, as though the speaker was concerned with something else. "For further punishment or retraining?" the nasal voice asked.

"Neither," said another voice, harsher and more guttural with a slight lisp. "Solitary confinement."

"Oh, that probably has to go down as further punishment." A stylus pinged on an electronic pad. "Sign in the box. There was a rustling of clothing. "Then what?"

"Dunno. Usually mines; all they're good for by then."

"Shame. Physique like that could have been used for recreational purposes."

"Except for the strokes, the tart—er, lady's not to be touched, not to be violated. Instant death to anyone who disobeys." There was a snorting rasp. "She's highly connected."

"Shame." A salacious smack of lips blowing a kiss. "That's me done, then. Take care." The voice retreated, and a door hissed open.

"Now, missus, don't be feared. Just doing our job, we've got to bag you. Dunno why, just orders. So if you be kind enough to just lift your head a little, we can put the bag on. Won't hurt."

Chapter lifted her head. She knew it would have been pointless to resist. A bag was slipped over head, and the microscopic linen threads tickled her nostrils. She breathed deeply to stifle the panic that instantly built as light and sound were obliterated, and she felt her hands and feet being released. Hot, sweaty hands turned her over and then lifted her off the table onto what she presumed was a levitation trolley.

She thought of Dix, her beautiful Dix. Even in the twilight dimness when she knew she was being caned she thought of him, she suppressed the tears in case they seemed like a sign of contrition. She felt the guilt that was wrapping round her, that it was she who had brought him back to be condemned. She could have persuaded him to escape. They both could have escaped to somewhere, and then at least they would have had more time together. In the darkness of the bag, she blew him a kiss and then gulped and swallowed. Tears filled her eyes.

Then she felt the hot hands on her, and she shuddered as they began to lift her off. Two hands held her shoulders and two were on her legs, but they were gentle and carried her for a moment and then stood her up. The leg hands let go, and the shoulder hands moved on to her top and pushed her gently down into a sitting position. Immediately the black bag was pulled up just below her eyes. She breathed in deeply.

"Close your eyes and count to twenty slowly before opening them." A sniff close to her face and the pungent smell of sweat. "This is so we can leave the room without you seeing us," the voice whispered urgently. "It's an order—don't ask us why. Just is, okay? Nod your head if you understand."

Chapter slowly nodded her head and closed her eyes. She felt the bag being whisked off and thought she heard a whispered, "Bye, sweet miss—good luck," but she couldn't be sure. After nineteen she opened her eyes, and brilliant white light flashed into eyes, blinding her. She screwed her eyelids together.

"Chapter." It sounded like Trunnion, but she couldn't be sure. She slowly opened her eyes, accustoming them to the bright light, and listened. "Love is blind, Chapter." It was coming through speakers, and the clipped, emphatic tone could have been Trunnion or Arcanum. "And being blind is dangerous. We know we can't stop you being in love, but we can isolate and constrain you from the object of your love."

"Am I being punished because you believe I fell in love?" Chapter asked, looking round the white glass walls and wondering from where they were viewing her. She decided that they were in front of her, given the way the chair had been placed. She stood up and turned the chair to face in the opposite direction and then sat astride it, hoping in some sense to limit her nakedness, her breasts and crotch behind the back of the chrome chair. She felt less vulnerable and psychologically stronger.

"Interesting." A finger tapping out thoughtfully, magnified by the microphone. "Believe?"

"Sorry, difficult to understand with the interference." Chapter tapped on the chair's headrest.

The tapping stopped. "Believe." A pause. "That we believed you fell in love, the supposition being that you didn't." A slightly puzzled huff. "A question?"

"You wanted the perpetrator—the perpetrators—if they existed. Those who wanted to destabilise our society, destabilise your governance of this galaxy, or discover if the promised land was reality." Chapter breathed in, no longer naked, no longer Detective Inspector Chapter Editor, just Inspector Chapter Editor, now Ice. "I delivered." She let her breath out slowly.

She heard the microphones being switched off. The white nakedness of the room gave her strength; there was nothing to distract her. She was on her own, and the chair was her only weapon, her only defence.

The speakers came alive. "Sometimes love obscures reality. We have two people who are in love—who we believe are in love. One of them, we believe, attempted to destabilise our governance of society, create havoc and mayhem for whatever reason. But we are being told by the other one of the lovers that this wasn't so, that it was an accident, a theatrical boasting, and is not to be taken seriously." The voice was offended. "Accident or malice has to be taken seriously. The consequences of either has caused—is still causing—a general breakdown of social order. It—"

Chapter interrupted. "I suggested a possible solution that might—"

"We have considered it and are taking counsel on it," the voice snapped. Then it said quietly and sternly, "Because you allowed your emotions to dictate your reasoning, your actions, we felt it would be unwise to allow you to have any contact with anyone—let me repeat, with *anyone*—who you might unwittingly persuade or advise of your possible solution. You will remain in isolation until we consider it appropriate to release you or to detain you further."

"Am I to remain naked? And why the caning?" Chapter asked sharply, swinging off the chair and standing, her white, unblemished naked body challengingly upright.

"Yes to the first, and standard procedure to the second."

"To humiliate and intimidate," she shouted, and then she stopped because she heard dead, empty silence as the microphone clicked and died. "You shrites," she screamed picking up the chair and throwing it angrily across the room at the white glass walls. They didn't shatter; the chair seemed to hover for a moment before quietly slipping slowly down to the floor. The light radiating from the walls began to change colour from peak white to soft mushroom pink, to deep bruised purple, to a final sightless and detached blackness.

Chapter felt very lonely.

Pandemonium. Demons were at work, and the juggernaut was beginning to slowly move. The long, dark, maroon front of house tabs were being grappled and pulled at to get them open by stage hands swarming below them like rampaging ants. At last the electric winding gear moaned into action—a victory won as the tabs, like a split skirt in the wind, parted and swept to each side of the grand stage. Then a victory lost when the winding gear refused to go into reverse to close the tabs.

Dix sat at the back of the auditorium behind his small communications desk with its brass reading light and microphone. He seethed, cursed, and screamed—but only to himself, never at the crew or any of the artists, whose fragile egos could take days or even weeks to mend. He was always calm and reassuring, taking any burdens off them so that they could do their best work. Unless it was an act of deliberate sabotage or spiteful jealousy, and then he would be severe in his reprimand.

It was the first day in the theatre of a bare rehearsal on stage—no scenery or set changes, just the various acts: chorus, singers, comedians, illusionists, acrobats, aerial and trapeze artists, jugglers. All of them until now had been rehearsing on their own, but now they were being brought together. Lrac was the lone pianist tapping out the music.

The bemused smile of absolute pleasure and the puzzled wrinkles of disbelief on Dix's forehead kept returning. The same physical expressions of surprise and amazement he had tried to suppress when he had been told—had been commanded—by the committee of the GEC that the Bix Bieder brothers had requested that he should produce a show in the galaxy's number one theatre.

Before he could recover from his amazement, before he had time to snap his mouth closed, he was told that there was a caveat, two absolute demands that he must take in to account. One was the time scheduled for the opening of the show, and the second one was that the final tableau of the show must be the one that had been unfortunately transmitted. Dix had nodded sagely as though considering the provisos before saying yes. He had to repeat the yes because the yes had been an inaudible, excited whisper. "Yes, I would be honoured. It is an honour, thank you, thank you." He beamed and gave quarter bows as the members of the board sat at the highly polished slate table in front of him. He felt like jumping up and kissing each of them but resisted. Instead he composed himself and cursorily read the contract that had been pushed towards him before signing it quickly with a flourish in case it was snatched away from him.

He squeezed his chin and then patted his hand over his shiny head and smiled politely before opening his negotiations. "I obviously will need more time," he said breathlessly. "The opening date is much too—"

A hand waved from the table, cutting him off. "The time is non-negotiable. The show *will* open on that date." The contract slid back across the table to the chairman, who tapped it with restrained exasperation, and a smile infiltrated his face.

Dix waited for a moment and watched the chairman, who didn't even look or acknowledge his signature. On the wall behind the chairman was a large, ornate, silver-framed painting of the brothers, Arcanum and Trunnion, smiling down at him. He felt it was their teeth and not their eyes that would follow him around the room.

He blinked them away and wondered whether he should mention the glaring admission that he had immediately spotted in the contract. He decided to come true, nodding towards the contract and hoping his beguiling honesty would bring future rewards. "There was no budget allocated?"

"It is open." No surprise at a possible lapse; his sloe eyes flicked at Dix's, and the smile sharpened to a slit.

"Open to discussion?" asked Dix, not believing what he'd heard.

The Chairman leant forward and whispered to another board member on his right. On his answer, the chairman returned upright. "It has been authorised as an open budget."

"I can spend what I like?" Dix gasped. The Chairman slowly nodded, but a thin, warning smile cut his face. "The best ideas start here," Dix said, slapping his heart. "If it doesn't start here, then you have nothing. No amount of money can buy it." There was no reaction from the members of the board or the chairman; they remained stony faced like well-licked bones. "I will only spend the amount required, of course." Dix could hardly contain his zeal and enthusiasm. He watched the smile morph into pursed white lips. "It will require more stage hands."

"No doubt."

Dix gulped. "It will require a larger repertoire—chorus line, artists, performers, orchestra."

The chairman fluttered up his creamy, leathery hand to stop Dix talking. "You have the authorisation to get whatever." He paused and leant forward. "Whatever your heart requires." A sarcastic cut of red smile appeared, and the other board members smirked in sycophantic appreciation.

But Dix still couldn't believe it. "I will require additional candle makers and specialist wick trimmers."

The chairman snorted and licked the smile away. "The theatre has electricity."

Dix's mouth opened and closed. He felt the flush of embarrassment rising. *How could I have been so stupid, so naïve, so crass. Of course number one theatres have electricity.* He grinned mischievously at the chairman, hoping that his gaff would be taken as humour. "I would like my own and my father's sparks," he corrected himself. "Electricians, to be found wherever they are. And additional assistants, scenic artists, designers and—"

"This will be acted on."

"I will let you have the names."

He gasped, remembering Chapter, beautiful Chapter. He realised that it must have been her who had made this possible. He wanted to see her, touch her, grab her, swing her round and round. How could she have known it was one of his most cherished dreams? He had never spoken about it; she simply knew, and that's why she was so fantastically special.

"Is it possible for me to speak . . ." He stopped and decided to demand it. "I wish to speak with . . ." That didn't seem commanding enough. "It essential that I communicate with Detective Inspector Chapter Editor." He wanted to hear her sparkling voice, but he knew he had spoken too quickly, too breathlessly eager.

The chairman looked at the board members with a puzzled frown of incomprehension. One of them, large and overweight with eyelids flickering like moths caught in a candle flame, slowly heaved himself off his chair, waddled to the chairman, and whispered in his ear.

"Ah, thank you." The man trundled back; the chairman waited and watched him slump back on his seat before he looked back to Dix, taking time to formulate his answer, his eyes narrowed into thin slits. "Detective Inspector Chapter Editor is, I am informed, helping the brothers with another inquiry. It is understood that she might be attending the opening night." He paused for a moment, looking at the other members of the board and then back at Dix. "That is all, I believe." It was a command.

Dix stood nervously. "Is it possible for me to send her a note, a message?" The fat man stroked the table with his pudgy pink hands and shook his large head.

Dix waited politely for the chairman to verbally express the fat man's answer, but his face remained still, passive, immobile. Dix nodded a mumbled thank-you at the chairman and the board members before side-stepping away from his chair and backing away to the door, trying not to bow but silently murmuring, "Thank you very much, thank you." He slid out through the doors.

Outside, he grinned and sniffed. "Thank you, Chapter. I will find you."

Then he gave a victorious punch in the air with his fist. He did a little celebratory tripping dance. "Dad, Dad," he whispered. "We're back up to number one. I've done it." He was sure that it had been something to do with Chapter, but he wasn't about to inquire or investigate it further. How and why didn't matter in this moment of time. He and the Candle Dancers were back and about to make a dream come true.

He still could hardly belief it, but he had stopped pinching himself. During the time when the cast and crew were being assembled, the scenery and scenic cloths taken out from the bowels of the *Auriga Lick* to be hung on the paint frames and be cleaned and renovated, he had discovered a corridor that didn't go anywhere. It was a small working space, a makeshift office, at the back of the gods, the highest seats at the back of the auditorium. He needed privacy, and the four flights of stairs up to it deterred most who might have disturbed him.

The floor in this tiny miniscule room was covered in small, screwed-up paper balls of his scribbled ink-splattered thoughts and ideas of his artistic vision and overall programme for the show. Pinned on the unvarnished wood partition walls were lists and photos of the cast, crew, and heads of the creative teams, constantly referred to and rearranged, from the grandest stars to the lowliest stage attendant. They were names remembered and hammered into his memory.

It was here that Dix composed, wrote the running order, and prepared the show's opening, middle, and end segments. The top page was simple, having just the names of acts or stars and the times and sequence they would appear; it was the basis for the printed programme. The pages after the first page were crammed with notes, prompts and cues, diagrams, blocking notes with the movements and positions of the artists on stage, barrel numbers designated for scenic cloths and lighting, cue points and musical scores, and inventories of requirements. Most of these details had been given to him by the various heads of departments. The sheaf of papers would become the show's bible, and as soon as Dix had completed it, he was fearful that it might be lost and had it immediately copied several times. One copy he locked away.

"Heads of departments," murmured Dix. This had constantly amused and delighted him. He had never, unlike his father, had the luxury or any reason to use the talent of this class of people when he worked the casinos. "Set designers, costume and wardrobe supervisors, musical directors, choreographers, construction managers, lighting director, musical director, casting director, stage managers." He laughed and then admonished himself. "Be careful, even deceitful. Give the odd lie when allocating their budgets. You don't want them to know about the open budget." He wanted them to use their imaginations and talents to overcome problems rather than buy their way out. He had felt an open budget would be disastrous and could lead to failure. "They have to be innovative," he said aloud, his words echoing along the warren of corridors.

He had let the first rehearsal stumble frustratingly on, and he watched as the sixty chorus girls floundered onto stage, legs kicking high and colliding with arms, the flying ballet tangle, knitting together and finally hanging like disused marionettes. He had heard Jollity's moaning that he had a sore throat, Babe Algol trouncing off because she couldn't perform with all the banging going on, and the chief stage hand running out of the wings and on stage, offering his apologies and excuses. The work had to be done, and he said it wasn't his intention to interrupt a great star, and how he loved the ridiculously high notes, how he would love to fuck her, but the time scheduled was impossible. Babe stuck out her tongue at him and swept off stage.

Popablu had sulked and complained that the follow spot operator was a buffoon, and he had stomped petulantly off. Dix hadn't forgiven him, nor would he ever, but he was the best crooner he could find, and the show always came first even though he knew that Popablu had attempted to kill him.

Xit had cursed and swore at everyone, but no one knew whether it was part of his act or whether he was angry.

Dix hadn't stopped it; he had just let it run. It was his way. No matter how rough it was, no matter how many tantrums, tears, sulks, or demands for him to intercede (which he always refused), he simply sat in the orange glow of the console light, scribbling notes.

Before the final curtain closed on this excuse of a rehearsal, he tapped the microphone. The sound echoed and pierced every brain and cranny in the theatre. "A few notes," his voice boomed out. "All cast on stage, please—and I mean all." He picked up his scribbled notes and the show's bible and then ran, skipping and jumping down the red carpeted stairs to the blue padded front of the orchestra pit; this was a routine that would continue throughout rehearsals.

While waiting for the stage management team to find and assemble everyone, he wandered back to the first moment he had entered the theatre and walked, slightly in awe, down through the auditorium with its blue velvet seats sweeping round in arcs, row after row, to the orchestra pit. He looked up at the cavernous stage stretching back into the darkness and towering high above him, and at the ramped walkways of the fly floors, the lighting and scenic barrels hanging still and formidable. He felt small and inadequate. Would he have the nerve, the inspiration to fill this space with a spectacular, lavish production that would make his old man proud?

The crescendo of feet skipping and shuffling onto the stage, and the soft murmuring of voices, the high-pitched braying of laughter from Irma (probably on being told a dirty joke by one of the sparks and knowing she wouldn't have understood it) brought him back to the fact that he was going to attempt to achieve it—no, not attempt. He *was* going to achieve it.

He heard Mister Christel shushing and asking for quiet, and he waited for silence to seep over the cast and crew. When pin-dropped silence was achieved, he announced, "Timing is everything. Timing makes everyone." He nodded pointedly. "You performers, crew, lighting, musicians, costume, make up, and designers all come together. It allows all individual talents, in whatever sphere they operate, to shine, and it will give us the ability to create a fantastic and unforgettable show." He paused, allowing the thought to sink in. "And remember and believe me, there is no business like it."

There was applause and whistles. He waited until it had died away. "We start. Overture and beginners please, in ten."

As cast and crew moved off stage, Dix headed slowly back up to his orange glow, and he knew the knot in his stomach that the steel coil wrapping his heart would never go away till the front of house tabs closed on the final night.

As he sat behind his desk, the burgundy house tabs swept silently closed. He knew the stage-management would be marshalling the cast and crew, giving them precise instructions, repeated three times, of where and when they would be required to be at every moment of the production.

He was getting thinner, and his belt needed another hole punched in it. The wardrobe mistress Ardnav decided it needed two holes. "You're wasting away," she said, and her lips pursed as she squeezed the handles of the hole puncher. "Not eating enough, not looking after yourself." She gave a despairing shrug. "What would we all do if you went?"

"Fitter than ever I've been. It's all that exercise." Dix laughed as she punched another hole and pulled his belt tighter. "How are the frocks coming along?"

"Darling, they're fucking superb, the most glorious I've ever seen. Would you like a peek?" Before Dix had finished his nodding reply, she had moved off behind the rails and rails of costumes, each one tagged with the name of the artist, dressing room number, and sequence of the show they would be required.

The hustle and bustle in the costume department excited him: the machinists with their heads down totally concentrating on the chattering machines; assistants with their dyed hair more colourful than many of the artists, carefully but quickly ironing the costumes and then sweeping them away to hang on the rails. He listened and laughed at their banter, snippets of gossip, rumours, and bitchy humour.

"Can you believe these?" Ardnav was brandishing two pairs of shoes at him, and the feet were extra long. "Xit wanted a new pair. Can you see the difference?" Dix shook his head. "One inch," Ardnav said, putting the soles together. "One inch. He said it was funnier, and you know, when he put them on, it was. Had me in fits. He's magic, that man, pure magic. I thought it was just me he was talking to, and then when he'd finished his little routine, I looked round and all the department was there. he'd managed to draw them all in, don't ask me how." She shook her head and snorted a laugh of admiration. "But then Mr. Jollity Strad heard about it, and suddenly he wanted a new pair. Said his lifts weren't high enough, and he wanted half again—"

"But the rake of the stage would be . . ." Dix interjected.

"Send him arse over tit. I told him, but would he listen, insisted. What can you do? They cost a small fortune. Anyway, I did as he'd asked, and when they were made he came down here, put them on, took a couple of steps, and arse over tit he went."

"Not hurt, was he?" Dix wondered worriedly who he would have to put in the line-up if the answer was affirmative.

"Not physically, but his pride took a knock. Nobody had laughed because they were concerned about him and rushed to help him up. He took off the shoes and threw them in the bin."

"Good," said Dix. "Two shoe gags in a show would be a tad too many."

"Well, I would check on that if I were you." She nodded and grimaced slyly at Dix. "When I looked in the bin later, they had disappeared."

"Shrite, all I need," Dix moaned. "An hour with Jollity."

"Give you an edge. Tell him you persuaded me to let him have Yar as his dresser; he'd asked for him, but I'd said he was already taken."

"Thanks. Why, though?"

"Well, he likes being played with before he goes on, bit of stimulation, and seemingly Yar is good at it."

"You see another side," Dix said, shaking his head not in disgust but in bemusement. "Always thought he was straight."

"Think he is, except when he's about to go on. Not like normal people, are they." it wasn't a question but a statement; she didn't wait for Dix to agree. "Take Popablu. What a performer, takes your breath away when he's on stage. But what a bastard when he's off. None of the girls will go near him, and few of the boys. Yar was one that could handle him, but . . ." She shrugged her large shoulders. "He's left with old Ytsrik. Neither will like it, and there will be tantrums, but what can I do?"

"Anything I can do?"

"No. That's my job—you've got enough to worry about. Perhaps I'll persuade one of the girls to help old Ytsrik, and tell Mr. Luvy Popablu it's his last warning; if he masturbates, vomits, or wants them to urinate over him or vice versa, he'll be dressing and wanking by himself. Now, let's show you a few of the frocks."

During the parade of the costumes, Ardnav kept exclaiming, "They'll come to life off the hangers." Dix thought of Chapter and her surprise—perhaps anger—that he had employed Popablu, and not only employed him but given him a number one spot.

"He tried to have you murdered!" he heard the condemnation in her voice.

"Yes, but there is no one to surpass him in the galaxy. He is one of the greatest, if not *the* greatest." It was the same answer he had given to Xit when he had challenged him about it.

"And that is all that matters?" Chapter's voice echoed accusingly.

"At this moment in time, yes."

"Then make sure you watch your back. That man is dangerous and evil; he can play tricks with your mind." Her voice faded as she leant forward to kiss him.

Ardnav's voice pealed in. "Tra la la, and for the finale." She clapped her hands, and assistants carrying beautiful peak white ball gowns with shoulder capes of spun silver, holding large white feathered head dresses spiralled from behind the rails. Dix gasped.

"Aren't they superb?" She was beaming with delight.

Beads of perspiration flecked Dix's head, and he brushed them away. "Sorry, I'm sorry, white?" Bright sandalwood yellow was raging in his head.

"The purest white. When they're lit, they will glow like star clusters." Ardnav hadn't heard the question.

"White?" Dix whispered then screamed angrily. "White?"

Ardnav's mouth dropped open. She gulped, totally confused. The gowns stumbled and snow-drifted into a heap. "White, yes," she whispered, gulping back surprised astonishment. "White—what you asked for, what you wanted." Tears filled her eyes.

Dix shook his head. "I asked for yellow. I wanted yellow, sandalwood yellow." Tears of frustration filled his own eyes.

She nearly said, "No, you fucking didn't," but years of training in servility kicked in. "I'm sure. Please give me a minute." She wiped her eyes and fluttered quickly over to a desk full of notes and fabric samples, and she began hurriedly sorting through them, finally finding a sheaf of papers, part of the show's bible. Then she found the note she wanted. "White." There was no jubilation in her voice. She crossed to Dix and handed him the notes.

"White," Dix read. closing his eyes and shaking his head in disbelief, then opening them wide and gazing up at Ardnav's tear-stained face. "I'm sorry. you're right. Please, my apologises."

"Thank god for that. Didn't fancy being up all night dying the wretched things." Part of the snow drift laughed, melting into movement. "Yellow would have worked," Ardnav said kindly. "If you want yellow, we can . . ."

Dix waved his hands. "No, no. White is wonderful." The soft sandalwood yellow faded, and he breathed in deeply and felt Chapter's kiss brushing his cheek. "It will be very beautiful."

But it wasn't beautiful. The wonderful white star cluster gowns, with their shimmering feathered head dressings, never appeared on stage. The show had stopped with a universal intake of breath that had sucked the life out it.

Up to that moment, thunderous applause and laughter had filled the auditorium, and each act had been appreciated. At the beginning, as the auditorium filled with the many dignitaries, casino managers, and mica mine executives, with their wives and consorts dressed in their finery brought from every planet in the galaxy, Dix had watched from his prompt corner spy hole in the proscenium arch, hoping to see his beloved, beautiful Chapter. When the brothers, the last to enter, took their seats in the centre of the balcony to ostentatious and enthusiastic adulation, a spot light especially arranged by Dix illuminated their position, allowing them to gracefully acknowledge the clamorous cheers and clapping before raising their hands for silence.

Dix felt sick, as though his heart had stopped beating. His body ached from the desolation he felt when there was no sign of Chapter, no sign of her luminous icy skin, her elegant and lovable body, her flawless and beautiful face with satin gold eyes crackling with humour.

The house lights faded, and after a moment the spot light on the Trunnion brothers faded. Immediately the first richly scored notes of the orchestra scorched, out and the long, tall burgundy curtains slid silently open. The stage was filled from the boards to the grid with what seemed to be hundreds of silhouetted chorus girls; mirrors had helped the illusion. On a waltzing chord from the violins, the girls moved in unison and the lights exploded on. It was a spectacular and tumultuous moment. The girls' timing was fantastic, and they kicked high and twisted round. The hydraulics worked for the under-lit glass stairs to rise up, and the male dancers dressed in red top hats and tails high-stepped down, throwing their silver topped canes high into the air. It was a celebration aimed solely at and for the Trunnion brothers.

Dix peered through his spy hole at them to see if they were impressed. They weren't; they were impassive, with not a flicker in their eyes of appreciation. Dix felt a wave of anger mixed with depression flood over him. How could they not show any emotion or feelings?

The act came to an end the audience rose up, enthusiastic in their ovation. At least the majority appreciated it.

Dix recovered and felt relieved, but only for a moment. Nervous beads of perspiration began to glisten on his head as Xit made his entrance. Could a lone comedian follow such an opening?

It had worried him throughout rehearsals, especially when Xit had refused to show or rehearse his act. He simply shuffled from one point to another for the benefit of lighting and the spot technicians.

Xit didn't fail, and he didn't insult the brothers, which Dix had been worried about. He was magnificent, his black comedy ruthlessly funny, and he held the audience with his every word, liberating them with his indiscriminate misanthropy delivered so intemperately but always with a twinkle in his eye. He was foul mouthed and full of hate but amazingly lovable. Their laughter and shouts of "More, more" dismissed all Dix's worries. He knew then that he had a success on his hands.

It felt good, he felt good, and he knew that all the acts that followed would be received with rapturous appreciation. After Xit entered the wings, a line of forty tap dancers thundered on, the shrill rap-a-tat of their shoes electrifying and mesmerising the audience. At a given, synchronised moment the line moved back to let a somersaulting

Mister Christel appear. He took centre stage and started to tap. The line tapped a response, then again and again, all in harmony.

All was in harmony except one girl. She was, sadly and embarrassingly, out of step. It was a discordant, jarring sound, and it seemed as though the audience, clenching teeth onto lips and grimacing, heard it before Mister Christel. He finally stopped and hopped on one foot, and the line of dancers behind stopped at the same time, all hopping on one foot except one, whose tap crashed down and echoed through the breath held theatre.

Mister Christel swivelled instantly round, his feet hitting the stage questioningly. He tapped to the beginning of the line and stared at the first dancer, a small and tiny girl, then gave a quick triple tap. The dancer responded, repeating exactly the triple tap. Mister Christel moved along the line giving a slightly different tap routine for each dancer, and all responded correctly until he reached Zelta, his daughter. He tapped, she mis-tapped, and he raised his hand and spread his fingers wide. He tapped, and the line tapped in unison, but Zelta was late again. Mr Christel shook his head sadly and waved his hand for Zelta to step forward. The routine of pretending to teach Zelta to tap correctly had begun. On the first tap in sequence, the audience applauded politely, and by the end of the routine, when Zelta was tapping as furiously and expertly as her father, they were on their feet stomping and cheering. When Mr. Christel swept Zelta off her feet, swinging her high and throwing her out towards the cheering audience, the audience instantly stopped with a universal gasp of anguish, till Zelta's ankle was caught and held. The strobe lighting helped to extenuate the few seconds of this amazing, impossible sculptural pose of a man, feet apart and holding a girl, arms stretched out, head held back, jet black hair framing heaving breasts, by her ankle at arm's length like a primordial tree.

Xit, at the side of Dix, smiled. Thrilled once again by the spectacle, the audience were silent, open mouthed and astonished, before they applauded. It was an explosive thunder that seemed to rock the building. Dix grinned at Xit and then clutched him to him; both were crying.

"No flying chairs." Xit laughed through his one-eyed tears at Mister Christel and Zelta as they entered the wings after the statuary third and final bow. Dix had stated that no one would take more than three curtain calls.

"For you," Zelta said, crossing to Xit and tenderly kissing his cheek. "You both." She smiled up at Dix. Mister Christel nodded in agreement, giving his lopsided smile and clapping his hands softly and appreciatively.

Jollity was funny, his languorous style capitalising on the pathos and sense of expected failure, which found a nerve with the audience. They appreciated him and applauded enthusiastically but instantly forgot him when Irma danced, skipping and pirouetting out of the wings onto a pulsating red lit stage. They cheered her, and she made them dizzy with twists, turns, impossibly high leaps, impossibly hypnotic somersaults, and passionate swirls of her bright silver sparkling skirt that spun high above her waist. All the men in the audience wanted her, wanted to feel her breasts and leave their finger prints on the luminous white, skin tight T shirt. They lusted after her, their femme fatale. All the women wanted to be like her, wanted to be lithe and beautiful, to have the sheen of her sexy, rangy body. She made them all feel marvellously and dangerously alive, and they gripped and stroked their partner's hands, thighs, and crotches, wet with desire, until she spun, twisting and turning upwards, high into darkness. The audience roared and demanded her return, but Irma left them wanting, teasing them to remember her.

Babe Algol made them forget Irma, and she sang with compassion and suspended time with her beautiful arias, denying the harsh cruel world that existed outside the theatre. She brought tears to their eyes and aching in their hearts; no longer lusting after Irma's young, lithe body, they wanted to be loved, to love, to care. But she didn't want to leave them feeling nostalgic or melancholy. She moved like a billowing, cerulean blue cloud sweeping down to the footlights and leant over to talk down to the conductor. He seemed perplexed and shook his head. Babe pleaded, hands together with large pouting red lips. Finally he gave way, searched through sheaves of music, and found the one he was looking for. He tapped his baton and signalled to the orchestra, Babe blew him kisses and billowed back to her chalk-marked centre stage. This had been rehearsed and timed—a theatrical trick to amuse and woo the love of the audience. The orchestra struck the first chords. (Why didn't they have to find their musical scores?) The happy, duped audience instantly knew the tune, and Babe sang the first words with joyous virtuosity, waving her hands to signal them to join in. With a crescendo the audience sang, except for the brothers. The auditorium filled and reverberated with a thousand voices.

It was a triumph. No one could match the old-style oomph of Babe.

After she had accepted three curtain calls and finally billowed off the stage, the acrobats, jugglers, illusionists, and high-flying trapeze artists swung and somersaulted onto the stage, holding the audience mesmerized. The giant animatronics of strange animals paraded through them and seemed to be from another world, another era. The audience was spell-bound and enthralled in a mystery. To another round of rapturous applause, the first part of the show closed.

The second part was given totally to Popablu. Dix knew it was a gamble, having one solo artist take over the whole segment, but in his theatrical bones and heart, it was one he was prepared to risk. The performance was astounding, chaotically violent and beautiful, compelling and spellbinding; heart-wrenching songs trembled and glittered with passionate, transformational scenes. Choreographed pneumatic sets turned the stage space into a dynamic, living organic structure, back-lit through trails of smoke and undulating dry ice. Popablu danced and sang in his purple costume shot with gold. The audience cheered, shouted, and stamped their feet.

Dix felt his face frozen in a wide, self-satisfied smile. The risk had paid off, and his murderer was now his performing monkey, delivering through his extraordinary singing and stage presence Dix's dream of being number one, the supreme showman. As Popablu took his bows, bouquets of flowers were thrown to him—again prearranged and rehearsed so that the audience would realise they were in the presence of a great star. Dix peered again through the spy hole, hoping to see Chapter. He sighed sadly; she wasn't there, still hadn't appeared. The curtains quietly closed, and Popablu finally left the stage into the wings, immediately collapsing. His legs gave way as he vomited venomously over the bouquets of flowers at the feet of Dix with a snarling, retching groan.

"If they could see you now," Dix murmured, listening to the applause of the audience and looking down at the crumpled, unconscious body. He bent down to turn him on his side and press his fingers onto the pulse in his neck, carefully avoiding the translucent excretion, checking that he was still alive. "Ytsrik," Dix yelled, and then he quickly apologised with a shake of his head and a smile as Ytsrik appeared instantly.

"Sorry," Ytsrik said, grabbing hold of Popablu and moving him away from Dix. "Did bloody marvellous, didn't he? Soon get him cleaned up. What a bloody star, eh?" He gently lifted Popablu up and swung him over his shoulder like a butcher with a carcass of meat, before moving off.

"He has to be in the finale," Dix shouted after them as they manoeuvred through the wings.

"No prob, guv," Ytsrik shouted back.

Popablu lifted his lolling head off the back of Ytsrik and grinned wickedly at Dix, his eyes sharp, sparkling, and evil.

Dix shivered, and a strange clamminess oozed over him. The pungent odour of scented sandalwood wafted into his nostrils, and he gripped the sides of the prompt desk and felt himself becoming breathless. Hot panic flushed over him.

A small voice kicked into his brain. "Mr. Dix, sir, it's the third in ten."

"Thir' in 'en?" Dix queried, his words slurred incoherently.

"Are you all right, sir?" the small voice asked speculatively, suggesting that alcohol might be involved.

Dix breathed in deeply and focused on the bible sitting on the desk, the words slowly became readable: "Act Three".

"Ac' 'ree," Dix said absently. "Ac' 'ree, 'ank 'ou." He turned his head to look in the direction of the voice. "Not 'runk." He laughed, swallowed, and flexed his lip muscles. "Sorry." He smiled at Geor, the assistant stage manager, and paused to compose the words. He said slowly, "Think it must have been something I ate—went a bit dizzy. How do I look?"

"Err, slightly woozy. Here." Geor reached into his back pocket and produced a hip flask. "Bit of a livener."

Dix took it and sipped. The biting hot liquid burned his tongue and the back of his throat. "Wow." He swallowed hard as his head cleared, and he sensed the flush of red returning to his face. "Right. It's a go for act three," he gasped, returning the hip flask.

Geor pushed the flask back in his pocket, gave him a thumbs-up, and scurried off.

157

Dix straightened his back, held his arms up straight above his head, breathed in deeply to expand his chest, and then lowered his arms as he let his breath slowly out. *I hope my gambit will pay off*, he thought to himself, having allowed the front-of-house tabs to remain open for a period of time so that the audience could see the building of the set, the final tableau. He wanted them to see the stage hands lifting and manoeuvring the scenery into position; see the lights being swung, lowered, and set; see the gauzes and painted cloths carefully lowered, stretched, and tied down before the tabs closed again. He hoped that the audience would appreciate what a transformation had taken place when the tabs opened again; it would give them a true theatrical experience, when rough wattle and daub, the grey scenery and stage would be transformed by light into something magical. He breathed in and out again, feeling slightly disembodied and knowing his stage persona was taking over.

"Right, ready," he said, steadying himself and doing a little jig. "On you go." He waited on the edge of the wings for his cue, and a slap on his back gave it to him. He strode out, and a gentle rippling of the tall burgundy curtains followed him to centre stage. Two spot lights, red-rimmed white circles, held him as he bowed low, acknowledging the polite applause. Then he stood up straight, holding his arms up towards the brothers.

"How we, our worlds, and planets came to be is shrouded in many layers of mysteries." His voice resonated through the theatre, and he lowered his arms in a slow, incomplete gesture, his attention now given to the thousand small, pale faces peering at him. "What happened in the confused and turbulent years; how many battles were fought against hostile forces; why our worlds and planets are barren and infertile; why the poisonous and gaseous winds rage, scratch, and tear at our very existence—we shall never know when or how it took place. However, we do know who laid the foundations for our present existence, who made it possible for us to survive." He paused briefly, allowing the audience a moment of contemplation. "The fathers of the fathers of the Brothers Trunnion and Arcanum. We have to give them our praise, and also to the ones who succeeded them, they who established peace between the planets, brought prosperity and stability back into our lives. We give thanks to the Brothers Trunnion and Arcanum."

The audience rose up and turned like a speckled, coloured wave to face the brothers. They cheered and applauded, and the brothers briefly accepted the adulation before holding up their hands, impatient for it to finish. The audience turned back to Dix.

"I am about to present to you how my father, my wonderful father, the great impresario Mandrax Dannering, imagined that our worlds and planets might become, after the last battle had been fought and peace was established forever. It is a tableau proclaiming the coming of a new era, a tribute to the Brothers Trunnion and Arcanum." Dix gave a self-satisfied smile and bowed low. The red-rimmed circles faded, and the tall maroon curtains behind him billowed and then slid silently open.

Dix was silhouetted against the brightly lit stage set: the twinkling artificial sea, the silver waterfalls cascading into shimmering pools of water, trees filled with blossom and fruit, ornate lattice work adorned with garlands of exotic flowers. He heard a gasp, an implosion of air into a thousand lungs. There was no crescendo of applause, which he was expecting. His stooped back ached, and hesitantly he raised it upright, perplexed. His smile became frozen. Someone screamed and then others.

Dix was astonished to see people fainting, collapsing onto the seats in front of them. Others slowly stood, mouths open and staring wide eyed, hesitantly pointing fingers at the scenery behind him and shaking their heads in disbelieve. Out of the corner of his eye he saw Sturm troopers running determinedly down the aisles with their guns held at the ready.

A searing, sardonic shout of "Traitors!" made him and the bleached faces of the audience look up and turn to the balcony. The spotlight snapped on, and the white beam shot out and held the brothers.

"That absurd theatrical pretence is what you put your money and faith in. Total make believe," Trunnion snarled. "You forgot who gave you life and stability, who allowed your existence. You stupidly, without any reference to us, our scientists, our astrologers, decided to act on your own." He pointed and wagged his finger. "Not one of you came to inform us of your intentions, or indeed that there had been a discovery of another world. It was a perfidious act that has devastated our economy, caused chaos, and created havoc and mass disobedience. You are all condemned for your stupidity. All your privileges have been revoked!" The white beam died, there was a smear of black velvet backs, and the brothers were gone into the shadows of enveloping Sturm troopers.

Then Dix's heart gave a joyous leap, with everything and everyone forgotten. Chapter was emerging like a flickering, newborn star. She was more awesome, more radiant than he had ever seen her, enshrined in a long, golden dress shimmering with freshwater pearls that caught on the nipples of her breasts. Her beautiful long neck and head looked as though they were carved out of luminous onyx.

She smiled down at him, a mysterious smile hovering about her lips, and stepped up onto the edge of the balcony rail.

Dix gave a silent squeal of fear and panic. His throat constricted for a brief moment before opening with free jubilation. He was amazed to see that she had wings—tall, burnished gold wings rising above her head and down to her heels. She teetered for one brief moment more before falling gracefully forward, her wings opening out and floating slowly gently down to him.

If Dix had given any thought, he would have known that she was being held by wires fixed to a harness weighted and counter-weighted, but he didn't and accepted that she was flying down to him. He remembered the first moment he had seen her naked; his chest swelled and his eyes watered with aching, raging passion.

Before she reached him, the Sturm troopers began shooting, blasting the scenery behind him, the fountains, the topiary, the line of candles. Dix stared at them for a moment, unable to understand why or when the candles had arrived. He blinked them away, hardly aware of the screaming guns strafing the ornate lattice work, tearing apart the shimmering silver waterfalls. The ribbons of fire burned into gauzes and painted cloths. He focused on her as she delicately touched down onto the stage, and her arms and wings swept round him. The flashing, exploding, searing crimson light and the crackling strident spluttering of the guns were blotted out, and he could only hear the soft, beautiful voice of Chapter.

"Dix, my beautiful, tender man. I have missed you more than anything in the world, in the galaxy," she whispered, curling him tightly into her. "I want to make love. We have the exclusive rights of the condemned."

"Here?" Dix gasped out. "Centre stage, in front of . . . ?" Laughter, joy and amazement tumbled together. "The wonderful audacity, it would be marvellous to show them our love for each other, naked and skin touching skin."

Dix instinctively slid his hands round her back to unclip the snap hook holding the flying wire from the leather harness strapped round her. He would free her, undress her.

He was puzzled that he couldn't locate the hook, and he moved his hands to her hips, surprised that she was on hip wires, which were only required if somersaulting was involved. He was surprised and amazed again that there were no hooks, no wires.

It wasn't possible, and yet he had seen his beautiful Chapter flying slowly down to him. He tried to squirm away from the smothering darkness of Chapter's hold with all his strength, but he was held tighter and tighter. He tried to shout out, tried to scream, but his breath was being crushed out of him, and he attempted to squeeze Chapter's hips. His hands met and twisted together, and then the harsh, pulverising realisation emptied his mind of all other thoughts. Chapter, his beautiful Chapter, didn't exist, had never existed, he had made her up, had imagined her.

He realised with a numbing quietness that he had never returned to the number one theatre, that Xit hadn't miraculously returned him to life. He realised with empty, leaden sadness that he had imagined it all, had made it all up.

He laughed a short, sharp laugh. "Always the dreamer." Then in a breathless, matter-of-fact whisper, "I have finished with life." He totally understood the simple words, the enveloping bruised purple darkness. An iron cage tightened, caving in his heart The noisy activity of his brain ceased.

"You have all said your good-byes, paid your respects." Xit's voice was soft, respectful, and commanding. "The glory has departed. The death of this greatest of all showmen wounds our souls, marks us with profound emotion. He was the heart of the Candle Dancers, and he will be remembered forever." He breathed out, as if extinguishing the flame of a candle. "It is the time to commit his physical being to the winds of space, the wilderness of the galaxy. We have loved and adored this man. We will remember him not for his body but for his mind. Our memories will hold his wisdom, his art, his supreme showmanship, his imaginative vision. Dix Dannering will never die. We shall not forget you; the manner of your death will be fully and rigorously investigated." Xit's voice faded into a whirring wind that hissed and moaned into silence.

The silver, metallic shrouded body of Dix is left floating with the rubbish and debris that had been jettisoned earlier from the *Auriga Lick*, now slowly moving away. In time the gaseous winds and smoky dark, gloomy dust clouds will sweep Dix and the debris up, will tumble and bind them together with nascent planets.

Many years later Estoppel Xit's body, by the act of coincidence, merges with the cloud. The strings and ribbons of his mind find Dix and forge together.

Hydrogen burns in a nuclear furnace. The mystery of star birth has begun, and in millions and millions of years the fusion stage will be the power that makes light, that warms planets, that triggers the start of life. A new planet will be born.

Our planet, our world revolving around our sun.

In the few million years of the short time of our evolution, theatre is born, and as if to honour and remember, a surname with the initial of the first name is framed and back-lit in every theatre: "EXIT".